P9-CMA-869

ALICE SHARPE

WESTIN FAMILY TIES

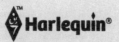

TORONTO NEW YORK LONDON
AMSTERDAM PARIS SYDNEY HAMBURG
STOCKHOLM ATHENS TOKYO MILAN MADRID
PRAGUE WARSAW BUDAPEST AUCKLAND

This book is dedicated to my mother, Mary Rose LeVelle.
I will miss you forever.

Many thanks to Kellie Waggener who shared not only her
expertise, but also her passion and excitement for the animals and
lifestyle that define family ranching.

ISBN-13: 978-0-373-69582-9

WESTIN FAMILY TIES

Copyright © 2011 by Alice Sharpe

Recycling programs
for this product may
not exist in your area.

www.Harlequin.com

Printed in U.S.A.

ABOUT THE AUTHOR

Alice Sharpe met her husband-to-be on a cold, foggy beach in Northern California. One year later they were married. Their union has survived the rearing of two children, a handful of earthquakes registering over 6.5, numerous cats and a few special dogs, the latest of which is a yellow Lab named Annie Rose. Alice and her husband now live in a small rural town in Oregon, where she devotes the majority of her time to pursuing her second love, writing.

Alice loves to hear from readers. You can write her at P.O. Box 755, Brownsville, OR 97327. An SASE for reply is appreciated.

Books by Alice Sharpe

HARLEQUIN INTRIGUE

*Dead Ringer
‡Skye Brother Babies
†Open Sky Ranch

CAST OF CHARACTERS

Cody Westin—The oldest of the Westin brothers, he thinks he knows why Cassie left him but he's in for a surprise. Now he must not only plumb the very depths of his heart to understand himself, but also foil the relentless killer who is after her—and their future.

Cassie Westin—She's been living in limbo with a broken heart and an explosive secret. Can she can rebuild her marriage—or will her recent past exact an excruciating price on everyone she loves?

Vera Priestly—What does this wealthy, elderly woman really see the night she peers out her window into the dark?

Dennis Garvey—This rebellious teen has plenty of reasons to feel vengeful toward the Westin family. Is he angry enough to target the most vulnerable member for ultimate destruction?

Victoria Banner—Vera's daughter likes the good life. When that is threatened, she goes on the attack and it doesn't appear anyone is safe from her wrath.

Emerson Banner—He's been handling his mother-in-law's finances for years but she's on to his cheating ways. How far will he go to protect himself? Who will he destroy in the process?

Robert Banner—After his grandmother's death, this successful restaurateur begins to implode. Is his grief fueled by family troubles or are there other factors at work?

Donna Cooke—She's under a lot of stress, but there's one thing she knows for sure: what's hers is hers.

Bennie Yates—What part, if any, did he play in the events that resulted in death and destruction?

Kevin Cooke—He disappears the day after a murder. Now it seems he's everywhere but in plain sight. What is he up to? Can anyone find him before it's too late?

Chapter One

Late October, Saturday Night

Her new name, spoken in a whisper, woke her from a troubled sleep.

"Laura?"

She glanced at the clock as she reached for the monitor button. Two o'clock. Before she could respond, the voice continued.

"Come quickly. Don't turn on any lights. Hurry."

Untangling herself from the rumpled bed sheets, Laura grabbed her robe off the end of the big four-poster, fumbling in the dark.

No lights? Why?

Her employer's suite was through a connecting door, and Laura took the familiar steps quickly, concern for Mrs. Priestly making her heart race. The old lady wasn't well, and after the stress of the evening who knew what had happened?

The bed seemed to be empty. Fearing a heart attack or a broken hip, she scanned the Persian carpets. "Mrs. Priestly?"

The responding voice crackled with undercurrents of distress. "Over here, by the window."

Laura finally made out Mrs. Priestly's frail shape

enveloped in the chair that overlooked the riverside garden at the back of the house. In the daylight hours, the view was one of Mrs. Priestly's favorites.

But this was the middle of a fall night and not a typical night, either, not even for Idaho. A storm had broken earlier that evening, and all that was visible through the window now were shifting shadows thrown by wind-whipped branches and shrubbery. "You shouldn't have gotten up without calling for my help," Laura said gently. "That's what I'm here for."

Mrs. Priestly grabbed Laura's arm. "I think I just witnessed a murder!"

"What! Where?"

The old lady pointed a gnarled finger at the window. "Right out there by the fountain. Can you see a body?"

Laura peered into the night, but the shadows were too deep. "No. Can you?"

Mrs. Priestly craned her neck but finally shook her head. "No, not now."

"Tell me what happened," Laura coaxed, hoping the act of talking it out would convince Mrs. Priestly she'd been having a nightmare.

"Well, I just couldn't sleep. You know when your mind just keeps racing and racing and you wish you'd said this or you hadn't said that?"

"Oh, yes," Laura said, kneeling beside the old woman's chair with some difficulty. "Yes, I know that feeling."

"Well, I decided I could make it as far as the window without bothering you. You do need your sleep, you know. So I sat here for a while, and then I guess I dozed. I don't know what woke me, but I swear I saw movement out by the fountain, so I stared harder. It looked like two people. One turned toward the river and took a few steps. I think it was a man.

"The next thing I knew, the other person struck him to the ground, but when I looked again it all seemed to dissolve. That's when I called you, Laura. I hate to admit on tonight of all nights that I need Victoria and Emerson's help, but I guess I do. You'll have to go awaken them."

Every protective bone in Laura's body recoiled at the thought of involving Mrs. Priestly's son-in-law. She'd witnessed Emerson Banner sneering behind Mrs. Priestly's back more than once before tonight. And then there was the argument she'd overheard after dinner. Mrs. Priestly had been shaking when she finally allowed Laura to help her into bed.

"I have an idea," Laura hedged. "Before we disturb Mr. Banner or your daughter, let me go outside and make sure you didn't see a falling tree limb or something else equally ordinary. It's really stormy out there and the light is tricky."

"I know what I saw," Mrs. Priestly insisted, but a second later, doubt crept into her voice as she added, "Would you really do that for me? I wouldn't want you to get hurt."

"I'll be fine."

"We have to look out for each other, don't we, dear?"

Laura smiled and gave the old woman an impromptu hug. "You bet we do. I'll be careful, don't worry."

"Just don't take any chances. You see one little thing out of place and we'll call the police. Okay?"

"Of course," Laura agreed, sincerely hoping it didn't come to that. She grabbed a throw off the bed and tucked it around the old lady's thin shoulders. "I'll be right back," she promised. "Don't move." She was rewarded with a shaky hand that gripped her arm for a moment.

Laura detoured through her own room to slip on shoes and grab a flashlight, then hurried down the hall. The huge old house was very dark, but thankfully the steep stairs were lit by well-placed lights.

In the kitchen she opened the door leading to the back garden. The outside lights refused to go on—something that had happened a couple of times before since Laura took this job. At least the rain had stopped.

There hadn't been a doubt in her mind when she made the offer to conduct a search that Mrs. Priestly, still upset from the evening's altercations, had confused a dream with the images of the stormy night. But now a sense of urgency grew more acute as she hurried down the brick path toward the fountain. She shined the flashlight everywhere as she moved, illuminating the gloom ahead, anxiety raising the hair on her arms and tingling her spine.

The fountain was a huge circular affair that towered over her head. Atop it, a trio of marble fish spouted water. Tonight, the wind caught the water and sprayed it into a fine mist.

Using the flashlight, Laura investigated the fountain and the area around it. There was a broken paver near the base, but it could have been that way for years, as others were cracked and one was even missing. There was no sign of foul play, nor, miraculously considering the weather, any downed branches, though leaves and yard debris flurried across the ground.

The rain started falling again as she looked up at the house, zeroing in on Mrs. Priestly's dark bedroom window. Big drops splashed against her bare head and face. She moved her search farther afield and checked the gate that opened to the path running along the river, as she could hear it banging against the center post. Impossible to tell how long it had been open—the latch was rusty. Propping the flashlight between her chin and shoulder, she used both hands to tug it closed.

A figure appeared on the path outside, looming in the dark. Hands reached out, grabbed the gate and shook it. Startled, Laura dropped her flashlight to the ground and backed into the yard.

"Who's there?" a woman's voice demanded, and a second later a small flashlight flicked on. Its light hit Laura in the eyes, then lowered. "Laura? What are you doing out in this weather? Open the gate at once."

Laura bent to pick up her flashlight as she placed the voice—Victoria Banner, Mrs. Priestly's middle-aged daughter. "I'll hold it open for you," she said as she fumbled with the lock.

Victoria, swathed in a rain slicker with a hood, came through the gate like royalty. She paused as Laura secured the latch once again. When she spoke, her voice was sharp. "What's going on?"

Laura wasn't about to tell the truth, not yet anyway. "I was looking for your mother's shawl out in the garden when I heard the gate rattling."

"What would Mother's shawl be doing out here in the middle of the night?"

"I thought I might have left it outside earlier, before the weather turned. She may need it in the morning."

"We're not paying you to be careless. Be sure to lock the kitchen door when you come inside." And with that she was off, her heels clicking against the stones, the small light she held in front of her disappearing into the gloom.

Victoria Banner wasn't paying Laura, period; her mother was. Besides, what was she doing out this late? And why had her hands been shaking when she grabbed the gate? Laura shook her head and knew she would never have the answers.

As she was getting wetter and colder by the minute, she forced herself to stop speculating and turned her attention back to the task at hand. She scanned the rain-soaked lawn, searching the grass for a sign someone had been dragged across it or had crawled away.

"Laura?"

This voice came from the back of the house. Now what? She turned her light onto an approaching figure who carried a light of his own, and with some relief she recognized Mrs. Priestly's grandson, Robert Banner. She'd forgotten he'd come for dinner and stayed to visit with his parents, who also lived in Mrs. Priestly's mansion, something he did one or two nights a month.

"I saw a light out here when I went to close my window. Then I ran into Mother on the stairs. She said you were out here looking for a shawl. Need help?" He was dressed as she was, in pajamas and a robe the wind whipped around his legs. "You're very wet," he added. "Can't this wait until morning?"

"There actually isn't a lost shawl," she admitted. "I lied." She pushed long strands of wet hair away from her eyes as she told him about what his grandmother thought she'd seen.

Robert immediately began a search of his own. When he discovered, as she had, there was nothing to see, he took her arm. "The weather is getting worse. Let's go inside."

They hurried back to the house. Robert stepped into the laundry room as Laura fought off a chill that didn't have a whole lot to do with being cold. He tossed her a dry towel.

"I have to tell your grandmother she was mistaken," Laura said, as she dabbed at her face. "Since there were no fallen branches to explain what she saw, she'll want to call the police." She hoped her voice didn't betray how uneasy that thought made her. And then she had a thought.

"Remember a couple of months ago when I brought your grandmother to your restaurant for lunch? I took a wrong turn somewhere in the back hallway and ended up running into a guy outside your office. He introduced himself as your friend. His name was different. Taipan, that's it. Detective Taipan. If we have to contact the authorities, maybe you could call your friend and ask him to investigate unofficially so your grandmother isn't humiliated if she's mistaken."

Robert was a nice-looking man creeping toward forty, with fair hair and light eyes, the kind of guy who would look young his whole life. But what warmed him to Laura's heart was that he made the time to visit Mrs. Priestly on a regular basis, and that couldn't be easy coupled with the demands of running a successful restaurant.

"I have a better idea," he said. "I don't know how much of our family dynamics you've gathered since you've worked for Grandma..."

"I try to mind my own business," she said.

"Yeah, well, the truth is my father and Grandma's own lawyer are doing their best to prove she's incompetent so they can take over her affairs."

Laura had suspected as much. She'd picked up on several innuendos. She suspected Mrs. Priestly had, too.

"I know Grandma is well over ninety and failing in many ways, but she seems perfectly lucid to me," Robert continued. "Everything kind of hit the fan tonight when she got a good look at her investment portfolio. She accused Dad of mishandling her accounts. She went so far as to threaten an audit." He raked a hand through his wet hair and sighed. "If she insists she saw a murderer, Dad and that shyster Gibbons will use it to argue her mind is slipping. And if they get power of attorney, they'll call all the shots."

"But your mother and sister would never agree to that."

"Mom will do whatever Dad tells her to do. And Donna is great, but her husband has sunk all her assets in that string of auto-repair shops, and I hear things aren't going well."

"Donna is over here all the time. She's very sweet with your grandmother."

"Still, right now she has other things on her mind." He took a deep breath and regarded Laura with anxious eyes. "I don't think my grandmother is senile, do you?"

She met his gaze. "No, I don't."

"Good. You spend the most time with her, so if she was slipping—"

"I haven't noticed anything like that."

"Okay. Let's go talk to her together. Maybe she saw a couple of kids having a fight. If she's still sure she saw a murder, then we'll call the authorities. How does that sound?"

Laura nodded, relieved for his help. One way or another, Robert would take care of things now, which suited her fine. She wanted no one in an official capacity to look into the nonexistent past of Laura Green. She wasn't ready for that yet. A few more weeks...

They hurried upstairs, careful to make as little noise as possible.

Thursday Afternoon

CODY WESTIN had already decided this meeting with his detective in Coeur d'Alene, Idaho, would be the last one. Two other times he'd come running from the family ranch in Wyoming when Smyth dug up leads. The first had been in March, soon after Cassie left him. That time had proven to be a false sighting. The next had been a couple of months ago, only they'd found the woman using Cassie's identification and driving her car had actually stolen them. The theft hadn't been reported, which left Cody wondering if Cassie was dead or alive. He knew Smyth had a new lead, but Cody wasn't counting on a miracle, not anymore.

"I have a name for you," Smyth said. He was about Cody's age, late thirties. While no one would ever look at Cody and peg him for anything but exactly what he was—a guy who spent a lot of time out in the weather riding horses, mending fences and herding cattle— Smyth had a street look that made him fit in just about anywhere. He was dressed as Cody was, in boots and jeans, but he sported a Giants baseball cap instead of a dusty brown Stetson.

"I just received solid information that Cassie was seen at the home of a local woman four months ago," Smyth said. "The lead was a little late coming because the woman who stole your wife's things lied about when and where she stole them. Since the DA struck a deal with her, she swears the theft took place in Coeur d'Alene, so I looked harder at Cassie's background. Turns out her older cousin graduated from a very small high school and one of the cousin's closest friends married and settled here."

"You talked to Lisa about Cassie? She won't answer any of my phone calls or emails."

"I didn't talk to her. I snooped around behind her back. It's what you pay me for. Anyway, the friend's name is Emma Kruger, who employs a cleaning service. One of the women on the team that cleans the Kruger house swears she saw Cassie in a car with Emma Kruger. This is the address."

He slid a piece of paper across the table and Cody picked it up. This was his first time in Coeur d'Alene, so the street address meant nothing to him but the timing did. "So as of a few months ago, and well after the theft of her identity, Cassie was alive."

"It looks that way," Smyth said. "We'll know in a few minutes when we drive out there and talk to Emma Kruger and make sure this isn't another red herring."

Cody pocketed the paper. "I'm going to handle this myself," he said.

"Are you sure?" Smyth didn't sound too surprised.

Cody nodded once as he took from his pocket a cashier's check made out to the investigator. "This is the end of the line for me. If Cassie is alive and still avoiding me, then it's time to call it quits. I need to put my energy back into our ranch. My father and brothers need me there. They've covered for me enough."

The detective took the check, looked at it and then folded it in thirds. "If you find her, what then?"

"I just want to know what happened," Cody said, but internally, he was enough of a man to wince. *You know what happened,* he told himself. *You know why she left you.*

Wishing he was already back in Wyoming tending to business, he got to his feet and picked up his hat. He started to take out his wallet to pay for the late lunch, but Smyth held up a hand. "It's on me. Good luck, Mr. Westin."

EMMA KRUGER TURNED OUT to live in a very large, very white lakeside home complete with its own pier, dockage and what appeared to be a sunning island accessible by a walkway. Cody glimpsed this from the road that curved around an inlet of the lake. The driveway itself emptied out in front of the house, where a black BMW was parked in front of a closed garage. At four o'clock on a Wednesday afternoon, the only sign of life was a gray-and-white cat stalking a bird on a patch of grass.

He rang the bell and waited for a minute or so until he heard running footsteps and the door opened. A woman a few years younger than himself stood there panting. She wore black leggings and a purple racer back tank. A stretchy band circled her forehead and kept wispy strands of brown hair from getting in her eyes.

"You caught me midworkout," she said a little breathlessly. "What can I do for you?"

Subtlety wasn't in Cody's nature. He took off his hat and produced what he hoped looked like a reassuring smile. "I'm trying to locate my wife. I was told you might be able to help me."

The woman looked puzzled. "I'm sorry, I don't recognize you. Oh, wait, are you one of Nathan's football coaches? Laci's husband, maybe?"

"No, Ma'am. My name is Cody. My wife is Cassie Westin. Cassandra. You were a good friend of Cassie's cousin, Lisa Davis, back in high school. I have a photograph—"

Her thin lips compressed. "I don't know any of those people," Emma said, and started to close the door.

He caught it in one hand. "I don't know what Cassie told you about me and I guess I don't care. I am simply what you see here in front of you. A slightly burned-out cowboy who wants to wrap this thing up and go home to his dog and ranch where he belongs. Any help you can give me will be deeply appreciated."

Emma looked into his eyes, started to shake her head, then seemed to reconsider. She stepped out onto the porch and closed the door behind her. "I have a napping toddler inside, and I need to go pick Nathan up from football practice in about twenty minutes," she said, as she folded her arms across her chest. "The truth is I promised Cassie I would never, ever tell you where she is but I've been worried about her, so I'm breaking my promise."

The first flush of joy at finally having a solid lead evaporated and he stepped closer. "What do you mean you've been worried about her?"

Her eyes narrowed as she tilted her head and stared at him. "You still care about her, don't you?"

"You want the truth? After six months of being yanked around, I'm not sure how I feel except she's legally my wife and I don't want to see any harm come to her."

"Fair enough," Emma said. "Okay, this is what I know. Cassie was really strung out when she got here. Someone had stolen her old clunker with her purse and suitcase in the truck, which meant she lost all her clothes and ID and she didn't want to go to the police. I guess she remembered Lisa telling her I lived here now, so she managed to scrape enough together to call Lisa, and Lisa called me, and I went into town and got her and brought her back to the house."

"And this was when?"

"About four or five months ago. School had just let out for the summer. Cassie stayed with us a few days but she was restless. She wanted a job, she wanted a life."

"She had a life back in Woodwind, with me," Cody said, and wished he hadn't. He shook his head. "Don't mind me, I'm just kind of perplexed about all this."

"Well, what I'm about to say isn't going to help that much. See, my mother has a distant relative who has a great-aunt, and that great-aunt has a friend who lives in a small town outside of Idaho Falls," Emma continued. "The old woman was looking for a live-in aide because she doesn't walk much anymore. She's quite elderly, but I gather she has more money than she could spend in fifteen lifetimes and intends to live out her days in her mansion. Other relatives live there, too, but the old lady wanted some independence from them. Mom's friend made a few calls and Cassie got the job. I drove her there myself."

"That was nice of you," Cody said woodenly. He took a look around him. This was as close to Cassie as he'd been in months, but it all had a terrible sense of unreality to it. "So, why do you say you're worried now?"

"Because we worked out that she would call here once a week. Lisa asked her to do that so they didn't lose touch, especially now, and she thought it would be better to go through me because Lisa is out of the country on work-related trips so often, and Lord knows with two kids, I'm never gone, never. So Cassie just calls and says, 'I'm fine,' or something like that. We agreed I wouldn't call her."

"And?"

"And Cassie didn't call this week. So that's why I'm telling you now where she is. Lisa is in South America for weeks and weeks, so she's no help." She bit her lip before adding, "You know, Cassie never said a mean word about you, and she didn't act like she'd been abused or anything. I'm going to go inside and get you the address. If she's really mad when you show up, tell her I wouldn't have broken my word except I'm worried about her. You know, considering everything."

Without waiting for his response, she slipped back inside the house. Five minutes later she returned, this time with a yawning toddler in her arms and a purse slung over her shoulder. The door clicked shut with a security beep as she handed him what appeared to be her husband's business card. Greg Kruger, M.D.; a hastily written name and address on the other side of the card was of more interest to Cody:

Vera Priestly
210 Riverside Drive
Cherrydell, Idaho

Chapter Two

Cody arrived in Cherrydell too late to do anything more than drive through a relatively small community built on a river. The downtown area was old but gave the impression it might have become something of a tourist destination with restaurants, boutiques and salons dotting the streets. He made his way to the house where Cassie had apparently spent the past few weeks.

Towering and dark, surrounded by huge trees, the gingerbread Victorian nestled on what appeared to be a half acre of fenced property right on the edge of a river. The rest of the neighborhood was equally scenic, though none of the surrounding houses had such large lots or were half as big.

He drove past twice, wondering if Cassie was in there, wishing it wasn't too late to ring the bell. For a second or two he thought about rousing the household anyway, demanding to see his wife, but he knew he wouldn't do it. Showing up on Cassie's doorstep was going to catch her off guard and no doubt create a scene. Stuff like that was best left for the light of day.

He found himself a motel room a few blocks away and tried reading, but it was no good; the words of the novel barely imprinted themselves on his brain. He finally turned off the light, but then he found himself checking the glowing numbers on the bedside clock every few minutes.

Why hadn't Cassie checked in with Emma Kruger? The obvious answer was Cassie's cousin Lisa got wind a detective was asking questions about her. Lisa could have alerted Cassie directly before leaving for South America. If that happened, Cassie would already be gone and he'd be too late.

He awoke at eleven the next morning and bolted out of bed like a horse with a burr under its saddle, appalled he'd overslept on this of all mornings. He took a shower and put on clean clothes while drinking a cup of the coffee he made in his own room. The motel coffee made the stuff he brewed in a pan over a campfire taste like gourmet.

He paused as he picked up the small black box that he'd been carrying in his pocket. Popping open the lid, he studied the contents for a moment, then snapped the lid shut. Leaving it on the dresser, he went back for it at the last moment and slipped it in with his loose change. It wasn't a bribe, it was a promise. All he had to do was find Cassie.

Back in the truck, he drove to the house again.

What a difference a few hours made.

The driveway and street on both sides were now jammed with cars. A few people could be seen standing out on the large porch—they appeared to be smokers relegated to the chill of October to feed their habit.

Cody found a parking spot a few blocks away and walked back to the house. He looked the place over as he threaded his way between the parked cars in the driveway. It had to cost a fortune to keep a mansion like this one operating, but there were signs maintenance had slipped. The house needed painting, for instance.

Plants had overgrown the landscaper's original vision and weeds grew in the sidewalk cracks.

There were two smokers on the front porch and they both nodded at him. As he climbed the short flight of stairs, the front door opened and a woman and man came out. The man held the door open for Cody so Cody decided to go with the flow.

The inside of the house gave the same impression as the outside: elegance and expense slightly worn around the edges. The foyer was crowded with people dressed in dark colors, all holding something to eat or drink, all ignoring him after a cursory glance. By the preponderance of dark clothes and hushed conversations, Cody thought it pretty likely somebody had died.

The motel coffee burned his gut like cheap whiskey. *Please don't let it be Cassie. Anything but that.* He chose a man standing alone to sidle up to. "Excuse me. Do you know—"

"Emerson and Victoria are in the parlor," the man said, moving off to talk to a woman who had motioned to him. Cody had no idea who Emerson and Victoria might be, but guessing they were connected with this house in some way, he moved in the indicated direction, entering another equally crowded room.

Through the sea of bodies, he spotted an athletic-looking middle-aged woman seated on a brocaded sofa, her graying hair falling softly over her forehead. She was surrounded by other women, one of whom patted her hand. A man of about the same vintage stood off by a window, alone.

There was something about the two that linked them in Cody's mind, a certain air of aloofness mixed with privilege. They were extremely well-dressed in tailored dark suits, their grooming beyond reproach. Both looked like they spent a lot of time on a tennis court or golf course.

A uniformed woman wearing an apron and carrying a tray, asked if he would like a canapé and started naming the offerings in a broad Cockney accent.

"No thanks," he interrupted, adding quickly, "Do you know the woman who owns this house? Her name is Vera Priestly."

"*Know* her? Oh, you mean, *did* I know her," she said. "I worked for her for five years, now, didn't I? It's shocking what happened to her."

"What exactly happened?" he asked.

She cocked her head to one side as her voice fell to an ominous hush. "You don't know? Oh, now, mister, it's terrible. Mrs. Priestly weren't all fur coats and no knickers, if you take my meaning. She was a lady through and through. You ask me it was that new girl who took over for me. Run me out of a posh job, she did, and her being all—"

"Bridget? I think some of our other guests may need attention," the man Cody had noticed by the window said. He'd approached so quietly he caught both the maid and Cody off guard. The maid immediately dipped her head and scurried off. The man looked down his patrician nose at Cody, which wasn't easy as Cody was easily five or six inches taller. "I'm afraid I don't recognize you," he said. "I'm Emerson Banner. Exactly how did you know my mother-in-law?"

Up close, Banner's face was crisscrossed with fine lines, his eyes were a pale, icy blue and his chin was slightly receded. He was the kind of man that raised Cody's hackles.

"I didn't know her," Cody said, taking off his hat. He'd completely forgotten he had it on. "I just heard she passed away. I know this is a terrible time to bother you, but I've traveled a distance. I'm looking for my wife. Her name is Cassie—Cassandra, sometimes. I was told she was employed here to help care for an elderly lady named Vera Priestly. If Mrs. Priestly died recently then it figures Cassie will be out of work." He'd been digging in his wallet as he spoke and offered a photograph of Cassie taken the year before.

Emerson Banner glanced at it, did a double take, then glared at Cody. The old saying *If looks could kill...* flashed through Cody's mind.

"I think you'd better leave," Banner said, his voice as cold as Rocky Mountain snow. He tossed a surreptitious glance at the woman on the couch. Her gaze met his and she furrowed her brow.

"I'll be happy to go," Cody said. "Lord knows I'm needed in Wyoming a lot more than I'm needed here. Just tell me where Cassie is."

Banner's voice took on a vicious undertone. "Have you no decency?" he hissed. "This is Vera's wake, of all things, and you have the audacity to barge in here." He grabbed Cody's elbow and maneuvered him through the crowd.

A younger guy with a pleasant smile intercepted them. "Dad? Is there a problem?"

"Nothing I can't handle, Robert. Do me a favor and find your sister. Have her go sit with your mother, okay?" The next thing Cody knew, he was ushered out the front door.

While he couldn't begin to fathom what had brought on this reaction, he hadn't put up a fuss because people inside were grieving. But the front porch was empty now and he'd had about enough. He tore his arm away from Banner's grip and stared down at the older man.

"Where in the hell is my wife, and don't bother saying you don't know her because it's obvious you do. What's going on?"

Banner straightened his shoulders. "The woman you claim is your wife presented herself to us as Laura Green. I was very much against hiring her as Vera's caregiver. The girl was not bonded nor did she have experience or references, but Vera could dig in her heels when she wanted and she was determined to help this girl out. She'd heard about her from a friend of a friend—your typical hard-luck story. Totally inappropriate.

"It turns out my suspicions of her were right on the money. We caught Laura or Cassie or whoever she is trying to run off with my mother-in-law's jewelry yesterday. And today we find there are several additional pieces missing. Who knows how much is gone? The police—"

"Where is Cassie?" Cody interrupted.

"She took off in a cab that dropped her at a bus station. No one saw her after that, but trust me, the police are looking."

Cody couldn't believe what he was hearing.

"And not just for theft," Banner added with a tight little satisfied smile.

"What exactly does that mean?"

"Vera altered her will right before she was killed," Banner said. "She bequeathed one-fourth of her assets, which amounts to over a million dollars, to your wife. She even included a phrase that covered the fact your wife was using an assumed name. If any of the others contest it, they lose their share. How do you imagine that came about?"

"It doesn't make sense."

"No it doesn't. And that was just hours before someone broke into Vera's room in the middle of the night and smothered her during a robbery attempt. For all I know, you were part of it, too."

"Listen, mister," Cody said, stepping close and lowering his voice. "There's such a thing as slander, you know. Unless you have proof, you'd better watch your mouth. You said my wife was caught stealing jewelry? If she knew she was inheriting money, why would she bother? You don't make any sense. I can't believe we're even talking about the same woman."

"Though there are obvious differences now, as I'm sure you're aware, the woman in the photo you carry and the woman calling herself Laura Green are either identical twins or the same person. I am not mistaken. Now, please leave before I call the police. On second thought, that's not a bad idea. What did you say your last name is?"

"I didn't," Cody said. He pulled on his hat and turned. Behind him, he heard the door open and close. Banner was gone.

The guy was calling the cops? This Laura Green had to be some other woman, someone else who stole Cassie's identity in a more subtle way than using her credit cards and flashing her driver's license. And that meant Cassie's fate was still unknown.

He took a deep breath, unsure what to do now. Go home? Wait for the cops to arrive and see if they knew something? Cassie's fingerprints would be in the house if she'd been here…

Across the street and down at the corner, he caught sight of a woman in the process of turning away from him. Because of all the cars parked on the street, all he could see of her was from the shoulders up, but there was something about what he saw that spoke directly to him. Maybe it was the glisten of her gold hair in the weak autumn light. Maybe it was a glimpse of her profile his conscious mind had barely registered. Something.

He hurried down the stairs and the driveway, then had to wait for a line of cars to pass by on the street. By the time he got to the point on the opposite sidewalk where he'd seen the woman, she was gone.

He began walking in the direction he thought she'd taken. What had she been wearing? What color? He closed his eyes as he walked, trying to picture—

Blue. She'd been wearing something blue, up by her face, at least. A scarf, a collar, a jacket...

He was traversing a residential neighborhood filled with stately homes set back from the sidewalk. The leaves were turning, asters and dahlias were blooming. There were cars here and there, but few people.

After a very long block, the road hit an intersection and he was given a choice of three directions. He peered down each street. Two old people walked a poodle down one, the other was empty, and on the third a figure walked away from him at a pretty good pace.

He went in that direction. It was a woman, he could tell that much, and there might be something blue around her neck. He wasn't sure how she'd managed to get that far ahead of him.

What was he doing? Why would Cassie have come back to that house after the accusations that must have been thrown right in her face? Banner said she went to the bus station. The chances the woman up ahead was actually Cassie were astronomical and yet he kept walking, forcing himself not to rush her, knowing such an action would spook any woman no matter who she was. And the only thing he knew for sure was he had to know the identity of this woman.

She turned left at the next corner. He waited until he was sure she couldn't turn and see him, then ran to make it to the corner before she disappeared.

Too late. She was gone.

He walked fast now, looking closely at each house in turn. Still, he almost missed the door closing at the top of a flight of stairs that led to what appeared to be an apartment built over a detached garage. As he stood there, the drapes closed over a window.

The house that occupied the same property had an Apartment for Rent sign in its window. He walked up the path and knocked. The door was opened almost at once by an older man carrying a stack of books and a big set of keys.

"I'm here about the rental," Cody said.

The man handed him the keys as he stepped outside. "My hands are full, so help me out. Take the blue one off the loop and give yourself a tour, okay? It's the back unit I'm renting. You get a real nice view of the alley. I rented the front one to a little gal yesterday. You're welcome to look at the place, only don't bother my new tenant. When you're done, slip the key in the mail slot here by my door. If you're interested, my number is on the sign, call me this afternoon. No, wait, today it's my turn to work at the library until closing time. Better call me tomorrow or drop by the library if you want. Ask for Stew. I'm running late."

This was all said as Cody worked the blue key free. "Thanks," he said, handing back the other keys.

"No problem." The man hit the electronic button on his ring and the garage door rolled up. The garage itself looked huge, split into two sections. One side was laid out as a woodworking shop with a lot of nice equipment, a long workbench along the outside wall, and a heater for the cold winter months. The other side sheltered a vehicle. The man threw the books into the backseat of a vintage 1957 Chevy and took off, the garage door rolling closed after him.

Cody had no intention of touring the back apartment. He found the mail slot and slipped the key through the opening where it clinked as it landed inside the house.

He'd intended to show the homeowner Cassie's photo, but it had all happened too fast; the fact that a lone woman had rented the place the day before fit. There was only one way to make sure, of course, so taking a deep breath, he steeled himself for another heaping dose of disappointment and walked toward the garage.

The stairs were pretty steep and ran against the side of the garage up to a landing. At the top of the stairs, you could either stop at the door of the front unit, or keep moving away from the street toward the unit in the back.

There was no peephole in the door, which meant whoever lived here had no way of knowing who was knocking. He rapped a few times and all but stopped breathing.

And as he waited he thought of the accusations Emerson Banner had leveled at Cassie. Lying, manipulating, stealing, murder. It was absolutely impossible to imagine Cassie doing any of that.

So, if the woman he hoped was his wife was actually someone else, was he about to come face to face with a murderer? And if it was Cassie? Had she changed so much she was capable of these terrible things?

His heart jammed in his throat as he heard footsteps sound inside. "Who is it?" a woman's voice called. Impossible to tell whose voice, but the underlying tension rang out clear.

He mumbled, "Landlord," and in that moment a jolt of doubt hit him so hard it was all he could do not to reach out and grab something for support.

What was he doing here? Why had he pursued her? She'd obviously left him behind, and yet he'd moved a piece of heaven and a whole lot of earth to find her while all the while she'd known exactly where he was. She could have come home if that was what she'd wanted.

Or could she have? Had he slammed the door that firmly in her face?

The door opened, catching on a chain after two inches, and he didn't know who he hoped would peer out and see him. A stranger or his wife or maybe a murderer. Or maybe a woman who had managed to become all three?

The chain slid away and the door opened wider.

For one interminable moment, he stared into Cassie's startled sky-blue eyes and couldn't have felt more winded if a runaway horse had tossed him to the ground and landed on top of him. All these months he'd anticipated this moment.

But in the end, nothing had prepared him for the almost physical punch in his heart that came with the first glimpse of her face. The creamy skin, the gently arched brows, the too-wide mouth and slightly long nose, attributes that saved her from cuteness and transported her to true beauty.

And then his gaze dipped lower and everything changed forever.

The simple gold band he'd given her three years before still circled her ring finger.

What was new was the bulging belly beneath where her hand rested. She was pregnant.

And not just a little bit.

Chapter Three

"Cody," Cassie said softly.

Her heart had been beating fast when she heard the knock: for the past twenty-four hours, she'd been expecting the police.

Instead, Cody.

There wasn't a thing about him she didn't know by heart. Not the way one eyebrow tended to lift when he spoke, not the exact shape of his lips or the dark brown of his eyes.

And not the shock that flashed in those eyes as he took in her changed appearance and began processing what it meant.

This was the moment she had tried so hard to avoid, the moment she'd had nightmares about. The moment when he saw her condition and undoubtedly leapt to one conclusion.

She cleared her throat. "How did you find me?"

"I saw you across the street from the Priestly house," he said after a moment. "I...I followed you."

She looked behind him toward the street. "Did anyone else see me?"

"I don't think so. You didn't call Emma Kruger when you said you would. She got worried." His gaze once again dipped to Cassie's protruding belly and the silence between them stretched tight. "Cassie? Can I come in?"

Cassie. Not Laura, not anymore. "Yes, of course," she said. As she stepped aside, she once again scanned the empty street before hastily closing the door and turning back into the room. And then her gaze met Cody's again.

She'd wondered, of course. How would she feel when she saw him again? Would the magic between them be gone, a victim of their fight? She folded her fingers into her palm as she steeled herself for what came next.

But why, why hadn't she dressed nicer that morning? Why hadn't she washed her hair or stuck on some lipstick? For something to do, she took the blue scarf from around her neck and looped it through the strap on her oversized hobo bag, her fingers trembling.

He finally cleared his throat. "When is the baby due?"

"A little over a month."

His voice grew hesitant. "Is it…mine?"

"Yes."

"Did you know about it when you left?"

"You mean did I know I was pregnant when I told you it was time we start our family? No, I didn't know."

He swore softly, took off his hat and looked around the apartment. She knew what he saw. The place was a furnished dump, there were no two ways about it, but she'd arrived the day before in a panic and all she'd wanted was a refuge, no questions asked, four walls and a locked door.

"I don't even know where to start," he said, turning his steady gaze on her again.

How many times over the past few months had she scanned the faces of strangers, looking for him, wondering if he'd followed her, half-hoping he hadn't, half-hoping he had? No one else looked like Cody Westin, though, not even his brothers, Adam and Pierce. There were family resemblances, to be sure, but Cody was the one a woman's eyes strayed to. The perfectly balanced strong body, wide shoulders and clear-cut features all added up to a great-looking package, but it was something else, too, some sense of reserve and privacy about him that made a lot of women, women like her, melt inside.

Face it; he was so masculine it confused her. In fact at times during their marriage they had seemed like foreigners thrown together on the stagecoach of life, seeing each other, touching, but not speaking the same language.

"Do you know the police are looking for you?" Cody asked.

Her heartbeat doubled as her hands clenched at her sides. "I wasn't sure. I guess it doesn't surprise me. How do you know?"

"I spoke with Emerson Banner."

Her heart leaped into her throat. "Did you tell him your name? Did you tell him mine?"

"Just our first names. He claims you had something to do with his mother-in-law's death."

Talking about Emerson Banner made the hairs rise on Cassie's arms. "He's a greedy, nasty man," she said with a shudder. Those cold eyes of his had drilled into hers too many times for comfort. "His wife isn't any better. They know I wouldn't harm Mrs. Priestly. She was so kind to me. Did he tell you how worried she was the last few days of her life? Maybe I should have done things differently, I don't know. I've tried to figure it out."

The tears that welled in her eyes were unwelcome reminders of the stress that had been building since that night when Mrs. Priestly had sent Cassie to check out the garden. It had culminated two days later when she went to awaken the elderly woman and found her window open, a pillow over her face and signs of a weak struggle before she lost her life. The monitor had been disabled. Cassie had slept ten feet away in the adjoining room while Mrs. Priestly died.

"Banner also told me they caught you trying to steal jewelry," he added.

She raised her gaze to his. "You believe him?"

"Hell, no, I don't believe him. Of course I don't."

"What else did he tell you?"

"Nothing good."

She had the distinct impression he was holding something back. "Just say it," she coaxed. "I can take it."

"Vera Priestly changed her will the day she died. She added you to her list of beneficiaries. You're going to be a wealthy woman."

Cassie inhaled dry air. "Why would she do that? Who told you this?"

"Her son-in-law, and who knows why she'd do it, but it sure provides a hell of a good motive for murder, doesn't it?"

"Yes," she whispered. Yes, if she cared about money, which she didn't. Still, to all the people in Cherrydell, especially the Banners, she must appear a penniless pregnant woman living in the shadows and desperate for every penny.

"Talk to me. Tell me what's going on," Cody demanded. "Explain why a woman who didn't know you that well left you a fourth of her estate."

His tone of voice cut through her anxiety. "Wait just a second," she said. "You don't understand what's been happening here, and I'm not going to stand by while you speak to me like I'm a stubborn idiot."

Cody pulled his hat back on in a way always guaranteed to start a slow throb in her groin. "Pack up your stuff. It's only a couple of hours back to Wyoming. We'll call Sheriff Inkwell when we get home." He dropped his hands and turned to the door. "I'll go get the truck—"

"Cody, stop," she said.

He turned back to her.

"Just stop. You can't just throw me in the back of your truck. I'm not a stray heifer. We're going to have to have an actual conversation about this, unless you want to continue to ignore it."

"I'm not ignoring it," he said, "I'm trying to prioritize. We have to get you away from here. If I'm going to have a child, I'd rather it wasn't born in prison."

"If? Listen, Cody Westin, there is no *if*."

"I'm not the one who ran away."

"Have you forgotten why I left?"

"No, I haven't forgotten. But things are obviously different now."

"Because having a baby is no longer an academic question? It's a done deal so you're going to step up to the plate, right?"

He narrowed his eyes.

She sighed deeply. They were right back where they started, except now another human being was involved. "We reached an impasse, Cody, you know that as well as I do. I wanted a family. You wanted to wait. Indefinitely. You asked me if I wanted a divorce and I said I'd think about it."

"And you ran away instead."

"No, I left to think about it. I packed a bag and drove

away. What choice did I have? It was your ranch, your family—"

"Yours, too, Cassie."

She took another deep breath. "I know. But that wasn't enough for me, and you knew it when we got married."

"But then you didn't come back. You didn't tell me where you were. You just disappeared."

"That wasn't the original plan," she said, pacing because she couldn't bear to stand still. "I just needed a few days to think and make some kind of decision. But then I discovered I was pregnant, and after our argument I didn't know how to go home."

"You could have driven down our road. That would have been a start."

"And presented you with the one thing you made it clear you didn't want?"

"I can't believe this. I am not your father. I am not the kind of man who turns his back when things don't go his way. You know that." He narrowed his eyes again. "You didn't think I could change, did you?"

She stared at him a second, then she nodded. "That's not exactly true. I just knew if I came back pregnant you'd *have* to change, so I couldn't trust that the change would be real."

He rubbed his jaw as he stared at her, another gesture imprinted on her heart. "I seem to be in a no-win situation. All I really know for sure is you should have talked to me. I didn't know if you were alive or dead."

"I'm sorry about that, I truly am. I took the chicken way out."

"When my detective reported someone else was using your car and identification, what was I supposed—"

He continued on but she couldn't hear him over the

roar in her ears. He'd hired a detective to find her? Of course—how else would he have found out about Emma Kruger? The news that he hadn't sat on his pride 'til hell froze over as his father would have done came as a shock, and on top of all the other shocks of the week she felt her knees buckle.

And then his hands were under her elbows, supporting her, and his eyes showed concern. "Maybe you should sit down—"

"Maybe you should leave," she said, stepping away from him, holding on to the back of a chair, unwilling to sit.

The silence stretched on until he took a deep, shuddering breath. "Come home with me now, Cassie. Let me help you through the next couple of months."

"I know you want to help, but don't you understand? I don't want to raise a family with someone who resents me. I don't want this baby to be my mistake and your burden. He or she deserves so much more."

She turned away from him to give her eyes a rest. Looking at him was agony. To love him, to want him, and yet to know he didn't really want the very center of her heart, the essence of her life…

Had she always wanted things Cody couldn't give? Had she always been blinded by her own feelings?

"I don't know what else to say," he murmured.

"You've already said everything," she said, turning back to face him. "It's funny, I guess. I dreamed of the moment you would find me so many times. That you would hold me in your arms and beg me to come back, thrilled I was carrying your child. But you aren't asking me to come back to you; you're telling me I'm an obligation. You want me to come back so *you'll* feel better, not because it's what's best for us."

His gaze turned stormy. "I thought a lot about this moment, too, Cassie, and in my dreams you weren't wanted for murder while holding our unborn child hostage to my inability to react exactly how you rehearsed it."

She started to protest and stopped. Is that what she was doing? Her head began to pound.

"Face it. You've gotten yourself into a real mess. You can't stay here."

He was right. That was the crux of the problem. Not the baby, not their marriage or their future, but the murder of an old woman and all the events that came afterward.

"Why would Banner say you took jewelry if you didn't?" Cody added. "He must have known you'd contradict him."

"He asked to search my suitcase before I left. I had nothing to hide, so I let him."

"Then the jewelry was actually in your possession."

"Exactly. There were several pieces stitched into the lining. When he found it, I panicked. The cab was right there and I just couldn't think further ahead than getting away. I'd seen this apartment for rent during my walks and I knew it would be safe here, so I had the cab drop me at the bus station and then took a city bus back. I'd never felt like a fugitive before."

"So someone planted the jewelry."

"Of course. Maybe if I hadn't bolted…oh, I don't know. Maybe if I go back to the mansion now and talk to Robert, Mrs. Priestly's grandson, or Donna, his sister, make them understand, they could get their father to back down. I don't want Mrs. Priestly's money, I'll tell them that. I was going to talk to them this morning when

I walked over there, but there were so many people—I'd forgotten about the wake."

Cody shook his head. "Emerson Banner is aching to sic the police on you. You can't go back there."

She pressed her temples with her fingers. "Could you just stop telling me what I can and can't do?"

He swore under his breath and regarded her from beneath the brim of his hat. "One last time. Come home."

She shook her head. "Not like this."

He stared hard at her a moment, then closed his eyes. In that moment he was so vulnerable her heart ached for him. When his eyes flickered open again, she saw he'd summoned the Westin resolve she knew so well.

"I came here ready to give you a divorce if that's what you wanted," he said, his gaze straying down to her belly. "It's pretty obvious, even to me, that you don't want to be part of my life anymore."

"That's not necessarily true," she said. "I just need to finish this alone. Maybe you could return to Wyoming and let me think and maybe you could figure out how you feel about everything, too."

"I know how I feel. What if they arrest you?"

"You'll be my one phone call."

Again he stared at her. She wished he would hug her and yet hoped he wouldn't. Did he know he was one touch away from winning?

"We'll do it your way," he said. "Do you need money?"

"No. Mrs. Priestly paid me in cash and I hardly ever spent a dime. I'm fine for now."

"But if the baby comes, a hospital—"

"I'll take care of it. Don't worry about…us."

He stepped close and touched her cheek. When his lips brushed her forehead, she almost crumbled.

But she didn't.

"Don't disappear again."

"If I decide to slink away in the night it will be from this place and these people, not from you, I promise." Her breath caught as his fingers drifted away from her face.

"Goodbye, Cassie."

And then he was gone.

She moved to the window and parted the drapes a little, watching him walk down the sidewalk. It didn't take too much imagination to picture herself beside him, his arm wrapped around her shoulders…

Go after him.

No. She couldn't.

But she wanted to.

And yet she felt pretty certain he felt relief that she didn't.

As she turned from the window, she spied the blue scarf. She'd bought it for herself, surprised real silk had found its way into a thrift store. Now it symbolized all the months of loneliness and indecision she'd suffered, and blue seemed an appropriate color.

She needed a walk. Dare she go outside again?

Her hand was on the knob, she was ready to open the door, but in the end she could not face all that open space. Instead she twisted the old lock and, feeling about as big and ungainly as a house, sagged on the sofa.

Cody was gone. Had he said one positive thing about their baby? Had he mentioned love? She tried to remember, but the last half hour replayed like a bunch of jumbled words and impressions, and all she could really recall clearly was the fear of Emerson Banner and the touch of Cody's lips on her skin.

Exhausted, she fell asleep before she could think it through.

WALKING AWAY from that apartment was the worst moment of Cody's life.

He'd found her.

And lost her. Again.

And now, of course, there was a baby. *His* baby. He was going to be a father whether he was ready or not. Had she planned the pregnancy to present it as a done deal and then started a conversation he'd screwed up because he hadn't known the script?

No, she wouldn't trick him. Wasn't her style.

Cars were leaving the Priestly house, and there were a lot of people milling about outside. He saw Emerson Banner and his wife standing on the porch, probably saying goodbyes. There was a lot he wanted to ask them, but the police car parked in front of the house kept him moving. He took a circuitous route back to his truck, got behind the wheel and made a U-turn to avoid passing the big Victorian house.

He checked out of the motel, grabbed a bite to eat and hit the road. As he racked up the miles he grew more and more uneasy. Not for a second did he think Cassie had a thing to do with Mrs. Priestly's murder, but why did she say she could have done things differently? The murder sounded like a foiled robbery attempt, nothing else, so why did Cassie say the old lady had been worried for days? He'd been so caught up in trying to get Cassie back into his life that he'd neglected to ask some pretty basic questions.

His thoughts immediately circled back to their baby. How did he feel about becoming a father? *Unprepared, that's how.* Three hours ago, he hadn't even had a wife or at least one he was sure was alive…

The afternoon wore on, and he tried to comfort himself with the knowledge he'd be home soon. Cattle market was over. Despite a tumultuous year, they'd done well; Adam's conversion to an organic herd was paying off. They'd been able to stow away an excellent store of hay and grain for the coming winter. Now there were several miles of fencing along the main drive that needed to be restrung before winter, but his brother Pierce was a whiz at that and for the first time in many, many years, he was once again ranching on the Open Sky. And then there were the upcoming weddings...

What kind of man leaves a woman he cares for in the situation Cassie was in? So what if she didn't want his help? She'd claimed he couldn't change. Was she right?

Christmas this year would include a baby—his baby. How could he be driving away?

He suddenly realized he'd slowed to about ten miles an hour on the twisting mountain road and pulled off to the side before he caused an accident. Cassie's voice filled his head like one of those melodies that get lodged in your brain and you can't get rid of.

He loved her. He had since the moment they met at a rodeo, of all places. He'd been competing in a bull-riding event and she'd been there with some guy she knew from school.

Cody had been attracted to her clear-eyed beauty at first, then to the strong streak of competence and spirit that ran through her personality like a vein of gold through a gold mine. He had no idea what she saw in him. He was a loner by nature and she was always in the middle of everything. He'd grown up in a male household with a missing mother; she'd grown up with a bitter single mother and a father who ran out when she was a baby.

So maybe that was what they had in common—missing parents. But while he'd coped by closing himself off, she'd opened like a flower to accept everyone and everything into her heart. He'd asked her to marry him on their second date and she'd laughed at him, but he couldn't help himself. After that, though, she'd asked him several times how he felt about children and he'd always said *someday,* meaning "someday a long time from now," when he was ready, when he figured it out.

And maybe in the back of his mind he'd assumed she'd wait forever. Wasn't what they had between them enough? Why add complications?

Now he wondered, was she right? Had he been putting her off because he was afraid—

Afraid? Since when was he afraid of anything?

He turned around. An hour later, figuring his out-of-state license plate made the truck stand out like a white star on a black stallion's forehead, he pulled into the alley behind Cassie's apartment. He'd been away for four hours—it was entirely possible she would be gone...

He'd just grabbed the stair handrail when something about the garage window to his right caught his attention. It was one of those multipaned affairs, and where before it had been intact, it now had a red rag stuffed through one of the openings. He detoured to take a closer look. Sure enough, the pane closest to the interior lock was broken.

He pulled on the cloth, and as he did so, the unmistakable stench of the fuel additive the gas company adds to warn a user of a leak assailed his nostrils. This was immediately followed by the bam-bam images of glass shards on the workbench below the window and then the sight of the heater against the wall, its fuel pipe unscrewed from the stove, a crescent wrench on the floor beneath it.

He took the stairs two at a time and grabbed the knob, prepared to fling his body into the wood panel if it was locked. It was. He easily kicked in the old, flimsy panel, then followed the sound of running water and the aroma of soap into the kitchen, where he found Cassie leaning awkwardly over the sink, using the detachable faucet spray to rinse out her long hair.

He grabbed her shoulders from behind and she screamed as she turned. She was still holding the spray and it hit him in the eyes.

"Cody! What are you doing?" she screeched, as he pulled on her hands.

"Come with me. Now!"

"Wait just a minute. You can't—"

"There's a gas leak," he yelled, almost carrying her to the door. She grabbed her handbag in passing and went with him willingly then, and somehow the two of them flew down the stairs in record time.

They had just hit the ground running when Cody saw the flick of a light through the garage window and registered a faint, audible *click*. A millisecond later, the whole building exploded.

The blast propelled them forward. He did his best to be the one who hit the ground first to cushion Cassie's fall. A second later, burning debris rained down around them, and he sheltered her as best he could. They'd landed behind a hedge, which also helped.

They sat up when it seemed the worst was over. The garage and the two apartments above it had been reduced to a burning pile of rubble. Neighbors began to come out of their houses.

Cody helped her to her feet and pulled her back when she started to leave the shelter of the hedge. Who knew if the bomber lay in wait? They stood there a moment, gasping at the destruction. Then he turned her to face him, pushing a tangle of wet hair away from her eyes. "Someone rigged that heater, Cassie. My God, someone tried to kill you."

"I hear sirens," she said. "We have to get out of here."

"But the police—"

"No, Cody, I don't want to talk to the police. All the questions I can't answer, the jewelry and everything— Please, I can't face that right now. I just want to get out of Cherrydell."

He stared down at her, at war with himself. They should stay long enough to report what happened and face things head-on. But that wasn't what she wanted....

"Let's put our personal problems on hold for a while and make sure you survive to give birth," he said. "Come back to the Open Sky with me. We'll talk to Sheriff Inkwell. At least he knows you."

Eyes wide, lips trembling, she nodded.

Chapter Four

Cassie couldn't stop turning to gaze behind them at the traffic, looking for—well, a killer. "What kind of person tries to blow up a pregnant woman?" she asked, very aware of the quiver in her voice.

"The kind who smothers an old woman to death in her sleep," Cody said, sparing her a quick glance.

Every mile that passed beneath the truck's tires vibrated inside Cassie's body. Even the baby seemed aware that things were changing fast; only the periodic rolls and gentle kicks reassured Cassie that the blast hadn't harmed him or her.

Cody had driven them down the alley with his lights off, exiting by going through a driveway halfway down the block that connected the alley to the street. He'd driven slowly and methodically, while constantly checking the rearview mirror until he announced he hadn't seen any sign someone was following them.

But Cassie couldn't let the hunted feeling go. Someone at the Priestly house was targeting her and, by default, her baby. Would they be able to outrun that someone?

"Who do you think did this, Cassie?" Cody asked, as they hit a major road and he picked up speed.

She shot him a look, then turned in her seat to stare

ahead. Evening had given way to night, and there was nothing to be gained by staring at a bunch of headlights. "How should I know?"

"Do you have any ideas? Any gut feelings?"

"Well, it has to be someone in that house or someone connected to them, right? My money is on Emerson Banner or maybe even Victoria. They both made no bones about how much they resented Mrs. Priestly hiring me. Still, trying to blow me up? Seems a little over the top, doesn't it?"

"What about Banner's son?"

"Robert? Did you meet him?"

"Kind of."

She shrugged. "He was always nice to me, you know, pleasant. More importantly, he was great with his grandmother, and she just adored him. As for his sister, Donna, she's nice, too. A little distracted right now. Her husband disappeared a day or so after Mrs. Priestly's murder..."

"Wait. Isn't that suspicious timing?" Cody interrupted.

"Yes. The police were questioning Donna about him. There's no doubt Donna will inherit from her grandmother, so it seems possible Kevin might have been involved in Mrs. Priestly's death. But why go after me? I've never even seen the man."

"Face it," he said. "It could be any of them."

Cassie rubbed her arms to try to shake off the chill. Apparently misinterpreting the reason she was shaking, Cody handed her a sheepskin jacket he'd stashed behind the seat, and she shrugged it over her shoulders. It smelled like him, of the earth and aftershave, and it gripped her heart with its forgotten familiarity. "Do you think the same person who planted the jewelry on me tried to kill me?"

"I don't know," he said. "I'm still trying to figure out why anyone would do that."

"All I could figure was someone stuck it in there in the hopes I wouldn't notice. Then they planned to follow me and swipe my suitcase and recover the jewelry. That way I'd be blamed and the thief would make off with a bundle. It was really nice stuff. I told Mrs. Priestly she should put most of it in a safe deposit box, but she liked to have her things nearby."

He spared her a long look. "That's not a bad guess. Or maybe someone wanted to discredit you so you couldn't inherit."

"It's all about money, either way."

"It usually is. But there's another possibility. Maybe you know something about Mrs. Priestly's murderer, maybe something you don't even realize you know."

She hadn't thought of that. What if she did? Chills that could rival the Indianapolis 500 raced up her spine. She closed her eyes. She needed to calm down, take deeper breaths, channel peaceful thoughts to her baby.

But she was scared and, truthfully, not just for her well-being. Every mile took her closer to the Open Sky Ranch and the life she'd abandoned.

She opened her eyes and stared straight ahead, trying to think, but the headlights drilled through the darkness ahead, creating a tunnel effect. There was the feeling if they kept going long enough, she would wind up where she'd been born and raised, in Cheyenne, clear across the state, a child again...

Back to the small house on Elder Street. Back to her astringent mother and the one treasured photograph she had of the man who had fathered her but had run off right after her birth.

"No," she said, and hadn't realized she'd spoken aloud until Cody cleared his throat.

"What?" he asked.

"Nothing," she mumbled. Her father was gone, her mother was dead, the house had probably been razed in favor of a shopping mall.

They entered Woodwind a few minutes later. Less than an hour to the ranch. She would arrive home pregnant and covered with soot, her hair a tangled mess, her clothes torn and dirty.

And everyone on the ranch would be there with a million questions…

"Cody, pull over. I want to get a room here in town for the night. I can't go back like this. I can't face your family yet."

He'd pulled the truck over when she asked. She hadn't missed his quick glance into the rearview mirror, and she assumed it was to see if anyone behind them had also pulled over. She'd checked the side mirror herself.

"There's a convention in town," Cody said, pointing at the Welcome Wyoming Square Dancers! sign on the No Vacancy hotel billboard in front of them.

"There must be a room somewhere. I need to clean up before, well—"

"Okay, I understand. There have been some changes at the ranch you need to know about, too."

"Your father? He's okay, isn't he? And Adam?"

"Yeah, they're good. Dad's knee is better—the limp is all but gone. And Adam's shoulder was wounded, but it's mended now. He has other news, though."

"And Bonnie? How is Bonnie?"

He laughed softly. "She's fine. Follows me around

everywhere but I think she's looking for you. She may technically be my dog, but we both know where her heart is. No, trust me, the changes are good. Let's check for a room on the outskirts, away from the convention center."

"Sounds like a plan."

They finally found a Vacancy sign displayed at the Woodwind Inn, located near a shopping plaza that was currently closed. Cody parked directly under the overhead lights and unnecessarily reminded Cassie to lock the doors of the truck behind him while he went inside and registered.

She locked the doors and scanned the shadows, her gaze returning at once to the strong, retreating figure of her husband.

Was it too late for them? Had her pride cost her a husband? Worse, had it cost her child a complete family?

She suddenly realized she'd been scratching her head and it wasn't because of deep thoughts. Caked soap and ash—what a sight she must be. Although she was pretty sure she'd left her brush beside the sink, didn't she have a comb somewhere?

She flicked on the cab light and opened her hobo bag. She found the comb after a little digging. She also found a half of a candy bar and realized how hungry she was—had Cody forgotten about dinner? She knew she had, but now she was suddenly ravenous and quickly devoured a few bites of chocolate and peanuts.

Patting around inside for the snack package of crackers she was almost positive she had, she detected something bumpy on the zippered side and angled the bag toward the light to see what it was.

She saw nothing and was about to investigate further

when Cody beeped the locks open and once again slid behind the wheel.

"They only had one room," he said, as he handed her a small courtesy package that included a toothbrush and toothpaste. "I think that's better anyway. Considering everything, I mean."

"One room is all we need," she said, ignoring the flutter in her stomach at the thought of hanging out all alone with him in a small room with no diversions. Still, that was better than laying awake all night by herself waiting for someone to break down the door and throw a hand grenade into her room....

JUDGING FROM THE UNEASY glances the girl at the front desk had thrown at him as he registered, Cody had to assume he looked as charred and tired as Cassie did.

The room was unexpectedly nice, with lots of extras like fluffy linens and even a small gas fireplace, which he ignited as Cassie took the first shower. He dug his novel out of his duffel and sat near the gas fire, the flickering flames immediately reminding him of the aftermath of the explosion.

Setting the book aside, he dug the small jewelry box out of his pocket and opened it again. Should he give it to her?

He could have lost her today, finally and irrevocably. And he could have lost a son or daughter he'd known about for less than twelve hours.

Who would try to kill Cassie and why? He needed to know what she knew—why was the old lady upset before her death? A premonition? And why did Cassie say she wondered if she should have done things differently? What, exactly?

He was so wrapped up in his thoughts he didn't hear

the shower go off and was surprised when the door opened and Cassie emerged, a towel wrapped around her head, a white robe, compliments of the inn, belted above the baby bump.

His hand closed around the little box and he slipped it into his pocket as he got to his feet. With everything that had happened, the miracle of being in the same room with Cassie was hard to grasp. For several seconds he just stood there staring at her until he finally mumbled, "I'll take a short shower, then we can hit the hay."

"What about dinner? Aren't you hungry?"

He hadn't thought about food. "Not particularly, but let me clean up and we'll go get you something—"

"No. I was hungry earlier, now I'm too tired to eat. I'll make up for it at breakfast."

He stared at her a second longer, then took himself off to the shower where he could bury his confusion under a deluge of very hot water.

AFTER COMBING OUT her hair, Cassie upended her purse on the bed and watched as everything she owned spilled out on the bedspread.

Okay, that wasn't true. She'd left tons of stuff at the ranch. Cody had probably boxed it all up and stored it, but her clothes and keepsakes would all be there somewhere. Things she'd missed at first, like old photos. Things she'd eventually stopped missing as the miracle of creating a new life took precedence over everything else.

The bag was empty and yet still felt hefty.

She patted it down again. There was something hard and lumpy inside the lining. In fact, when she held the bag under the lamp, she could see where the lining had been stitched with a different color thread. It was possible it had been done by the previous owner—after the theft a few months before, she'd bought this bag at a thrift store.

However, in light of what had shown up stitched inside her suitcase...

A pair of cuticle scissors took care of the seam.

With a growing sense of dread, she pulled out an emerald, diamond and platinum ring that shone with such intensity it was as though the central stone harbored licks of green fire.

And that wasn't all. There were two other pieces: a ruby broach and a sapphire necklace. Each piece was familiar, as Mrs. Priestly had shown them to her. And each piece was worth a bundle.

The shower went off.

Not entirely sure why her gut reaction was to hide the jewelry, Cassie quickly slipped it all back where she found it. Then she carefully layered all her own belongings over the contraband, finishing just seconds before Cody exited the bathroom wearing sweatpants and nothing else.

A jolt of longing for him hit her with such force she was pretty sure the air in the room clouded.

He was towel-drying his short dark hair, the muscles in his chest and arms flexing with each movement. A flood of memories, all involving him naked and aroused, delivered another punch, and she took a deep breath.

Oh, the times they had had!

"You okay?" he asked, as he crossed the room and checked the locked door.

"Fine. Um, tired."

She put the purse on the floor by her side of the bed and, still wearing the robe, slipped under the covers and lay on her side, looking away from him. A few moments later he got in beside her, his big body steaming hot and smelling of soap and aftershave. She squeezed her eyes shut as the mattress burned between them.

The light went out and she lay there trying to figure out what to do about the jewelry. Why hadn't she just shown it to Cody? It wasn't like she'd taken anything. Oh, man, how was she going to get it back to the family? She knew the ring in particular was intended for Donna, Mrs. Priestly's granddaughter, and heaven knew Donna would treasure it.

Or sell it—who knew? The point was, it belonged to her now.

So, who stuck it all in Cassie's handbag? She laboriously rolled onto her back and stared up into the dark.

"Can't sleep?" Cody asked. He sounded as awake as she was.

She wanted to talk to him about the jewelry. She wanted to share her fear that she was being set up and it would never stop until a pair of handcuffs were snapped around her wrists.

The bed shifted. When she glanced his way, the ambient light that crept through the gap in the drapes revealed he'd turned on his side to face her.

"No," she whispered.

"Anything I can do to help?"

His question kind of hung there. In years gone past, the answer to that question was a hearty yes followed by an hour or so of unbridled passion. But this wasn't then; they were still feeling their way with each other.

"Cassie?"

"Tell me about the changes on the ranch."

"Well, for one thing, Pierce is home. Not right now, but he's moving back very soon."

Cassie's erratic thoughts were instantly galvanized

by this news. "I thought your brother hated ranching and Wyoming and your father, too, for that matter."

"Well, he came home the first time I left in a hurry. He got there a little while before a party of visiting royalty were due to land, and in my rush to leave I forgot to tell anyone about the visit. To make a long story short, he and Dad spent some time together but, most importantly, Pierce fell in love with the princess of Chatioux."

"He fell in love with Princess Analise?"

"Yep. And she with him. Turns out her idea of a dream life is living somewhere where she's free to be who and what she wants. I don't know if Pierce all of a sudden saw the ranch through her eyes, but he sold out his share of his business and moved home. They're getting married in a few weeks, after Thanksgiving but before Christmas."

"Wow."

"I know. And then there's Adam. He fell in love with our stepcousin, Echo DeGris. They're getting married, too."

Cassie stared at him in the dark. "You're kidding me."

"Nope."

"This is amazing."

"There are also people excavating the burial cavern at the old cave, remember, I took you up there once. There are strangers around the ranch now, cars coming and going, people with their own agendas. It's weird, but in an odd way it's also kind of nice."

"And your father agreed to this?"

"It took a little convincing."

She thought she understood what he meant about it being weird but nice. Nice that there were new people around, hustle and bustle beyond the cattle and the ongoing responsibilities of the ranch. She'd never admitted it to him, but she'd found the place a little lonely at times.

She saw the shape of his hand right before his fingers touched her face.

"And there's more, too," he said, gently stroking her cheek. He probably wasn't aware of the fireworks shooting off under her skin. "My uncle Pete is back at the ranch after thirty years of exile, but the biggest news is we found out what really happened to my mother. It kind of shook the world at the Open Sky."

"I can't believe all this."

His voice grew thoughtful. "I can't, either. But truthfully, everything happened in a haze for me. I was too preoccupied trying to find you to pay proper attention to what was going on right under my own nose. I feel like I've been trapped in a fog bank."

She swallowed hard. "Cody—"

"I just want you to know I've missed you."

"I'm—"

"I know, I know. The deal was we concentrate on keeping you alive and figure out our future later, right?"

After a moment, she whispered, "That's right."

His fingertips brushed her lips as he withdrew his hand. "We need to talk about what happened at the Priestly house. The old lady's death must have a direct link to what's happening to you."

"I'm not sure things are related," she said, and her voice sounded wobbly. Too many emotions too fast.

"Will you talk about it?"

"Maybe it could wait until morning."

"Okay. Sure." He turned back on his other side while she, feeling like a beached whale, stayed on her back. The small fortune in jewelry sent out pulsing vibes she was surprised Cody couldn't feel.

Or maybe the vibes were coming from her. She hadn't even thought about sex in six months, and now it was practically all she could think about.

That and the pain in Cody's voice.

And then another thought struck like a lightning bolt. Someone had to have taken everything out of her purse in order to open the lining and hide the jewels. That meant someone could have looked in the zippered compartment in the lining and found the tiny slip of paper with Cody's name and phone number. She'd stuck it in there as a precaution in case something happened to her but not the baby. She'd wanted to make sure her child would have a family just in case—

Cody had mentioned telling the Banners his first name. It wouldn't take a genius for that someone to link him to the name Cody Westin on the paper, and presto—they'd know her last name.

Someone could know who she really was.

Or maybe that someone hadn't looked in the zippered pocket or written down the phone number—who knew?

She lay there for what seemed like a lifetime, sure she would never sleep, until she suddenly awoke to find Cody seated on a chair, pulling on his boots. Sunlight peeked through the crack in the curtains.

He offered to bring breakfast back to the room. Cassie appreciated the offer; she wasn't anxious to come face to face with old acquaintances just yet, and Woodwind was, after all, the closest town to the Open Sky Ranch. She'd been shopping in it on a regular basis up until six months ago.

But she had another motive for asking for the asparagus frittata she knew Cody would have to drive across town to find. Before she'd fallen asleep the night before, she'd finally had a brainstorm.

"Lock the doors, stay away from the windows," Cody implored before driving away. As soon as he was gone, she opened his duffel bag and dug through looking for sweats. She was in a hurry—

But her fingers came into contact with a small velvet box, and she extracted it with wide eyes. Was there a woman alive who could withstand the temptation to peek inside such a thing? She knew she couldn't...

"Holy-moley," she whispered, as diamonds and emeralds dazzled her eyes. There were six of each, staggered one after the other, each embraced in a ribbon of white gold leaves. An eternity ring, she realized, delicate and jaw-dropping at the same time.

What was Cody doing with something like this? She turned the box over and saw a gold sticker on the bottom—it had come from Woodwind's one designer-jewelry store, Wild Iris. It must have cost him a bundle.

Had he bought it for her? The emeralds could represent May, the month they were married. Had he bought it for their anniversary, which she'd missed? Or was it intended for someone else?

No, that wasn't Cody's style. So why hadn't he given it to her?

Maybe he wasn't as sure as he pretended to be...

Why had she snooped? Now she was miserable. She put it back where she found it and abandoned the idea of his sweatpants. She didn't want him to suspect she'd seen his secret.

That meant dressing in her slacks from the night before, which she did in a hurry. She would forget about the emerald-and-diamond band for now—didn't she already have more than her share of jewelry problems?

A few minutes later, she walked as fast as she could to the post office, which was just a block over. She'd never felt so exposed, not even the night she left Mrs. Priestly's house for the last time.

But no one stopped and talked to her, and no killer jumped out from behind a bush. Keeping her head down, she took the jewels from her purse. She'd wrapped them in one of the inn's plush washcloths, and she quickly stuffed everything in an overnight delivery envelope, which she addressed to the Banners at the Priestly house. She insured it for the maximum amount.

Cody would come unglued if he found out she'd done it this way. He would insist she give everything to the sheriff, that it was evidence of some kind.

And he was right. Undoubtedly it was. But she didn't plan to talk to the sheriff.

On the way back to the inn, she found a real honest-to-goodness pay phone and called her old landlord's number, which she'd found on a receipt in her wallet. She was relieved when his answering machine picked up, and she left a quick message about being frightened when her apartment blew up and deciding to move on, assuring him she was fine.

She also called Emma Kruger and once again got a machine, and she left a quick explanation of why she hadn't checked in per their arrangement. Then a quick call to her cousin Lisa. A third answering machine. She left yet another message, but at least no one would worry about her now.

Most likely the explosion would be viewed as a gas-leak accident. Most likely the Banners would forget all about her if she didn't try to claim any inheritance. And even if they knew her real name, why bother with her? With the return of the jewelry, the Banners would have no reason to hunt for her. And no one could really believe she had anything to do with Mrs. Priestly's murder, could they?

She just couldn't risk jail, not with the baby coming, not without making sure she'd done everything she could to avoid it.

She hurried back to the hotel, closing and locking the door behind her with a huge sigh of relief. Within a few minutes, Cody arrived carrying a newspaper and two bags from which the most wonderful aromas wafted. They cleared off a spot at the small table by the window and dug into frittata, fresh fruit and steaming coffee. Her appetite overcame her tension. It was the first meal Cassie had enjoyed in months, and in a way she felt as though she was emerging from her own fog.

He opened the paper as she split the last of the coffee between them. As he scanned the front page, she picked up the second section, and for a second it was like old times, them sitting quietly together, the day stretching ahead. Danger seemed a million miles away....

Her gaze landed on a grainy black-and-white photo of a recovery scene downriver from Cherrydell. A body had been discovered. Male, it said, identity unknown. He'd been in the water for several days, the article continued, cause of death as yet undetermined.

"Cassie, what is it?" Cody asked.

She looked up at him.

He gestured at the newspaper she held in her hands. "You suddenly got very quiet," he added. "Is there something about you in here?"

"No, not really, but..." She stood abruptly.

"But?"

"Let's get out of here, Cody. It's time you heard what Mrs. Priestly thought she saw through her bedroom window."

Chapter Five

He grabbed the newspaper as Cassie hustled into the bathroom to gather what few possessions she had with her. He scanned the section she'd been reading but could see nothing that would have spooked her.

He dumped his own things into his suitcase. Within five minutes, they were back in the truck, driving out of Woodwind. Cassie's gaze flickered between the windows and the mirrors. Her renewed nervousness electrified the interior of the cab.

"Tell me what's going on," he said.

"Is that blue van following us?"

He found the van in question by looking in his side mirror. It turned a block later and didn't reappear. "No," he said. "Cassie, what was in the paper?"

She turned wide eyes to him. "Let me start at the beginning, okay? Let me start with a rainy night."

She hugged herself as she spoke. Cody listened without interrupting as she related hurrying to Vera Priestly's bedside in the middle of the night to find the old woman seated in front of her window, where she claimed to have witnessed a murder down in her garden. He could easily envision the confusing shadows swirling in the stormy dark and the two women trying to make sense of them.

By the time they sped by the university, Cassie had

recounted meeting up with Victoria Banner out by the river gate, and then Robert Banner dressed in robe and slippers, dripping wet, within minutes. When the search proved fruitless, their decision to talk to Mrs. Priestly rather than tell the older Banners what was going on seemed reasonable to him. Cody would have done the same thing, given what he'd seen of Emerson Banner.

"That night, when Robert and I spoke with her, she agreed it was either her imagination or a dream," Cassie continued. "I thought that was the end of it, but the next morning she was agitated again. She made me help her into her wheelchair and we took a stroll in the garden. The weather was miserable, and I knew she shouldn't be out in it, but she insisted. Then she sat by that window forever, staring down at the fountain until she asked me to once again take her outside. It was raining, but I did as she requested."

Cody rubbed his face as he thought. "Do you know what Mrs. Priestly was looking for?"

"I'm not sure," Cassie said. "She seemed real interested in the fountain and had me show her a broken paver. Then we went back inside, and she once again took up her post by her window.

"Of course, by then Victoria had noticed her mother was preoccupied and asked about it. Then while I cringed, Mrs. Priestly told Victoria what she thought she'd seen. Mrs. Banner couldn't wait to get to the phone and call her husband. But Mrs. Priestly had a glint in her eye, and I got the feeling she'd purposely told her daughter, like it was a challenge of some kind."

"Where was Banner?"

"He took off early that morning looking like the hounds of hell were after him. I heard Victoria tell Bridget, that's Mrs. Banner's maid, that Mr. Banner had gone into the office. I think he was trying to find a way to forestall an audit."

Cody shook his head.

"Now this is where it all gets even stranger." She paused for a moment, as though organizing her thoughts, forgetting to check the windows every few seconds. "Sometime in the late afternoon Mrs. Priestly was still sitting at that blasted window when she let out an audible gasp. I was reading nearby. When I looked up, I saw she'd drawn back from the glass as though she was afraid of being seen. I went to her side to make sure she was okay and looked down in the garden below. Robert was out there, but so were Emerson and Victoria Banner. And they were talking with Judge Taylor and Bert Gibbons."

"And who are Judge Taylor and Bert Gibbons?"

"Oh, sorry. Taylor is a neighbor. Retired judge. He and his wife play golf with the Banners. Gibbons is Mrs. Priestly's attorney. A while later, the judge and the lawyer came upstairs and asked Mrs. Priestly about what she'd seen. It was pretty obvious to me that the Banners had asked the judge to talk to her, that they were starting a campaign to have Mrs. Priestly ruled incompetent."

"And that night she was killed?"

"No. The next day Mrs. Priestly had me call the attorney's office, except I was supposed to ask for a different man than Gibbons. The lawyer who showed up was a lot younger. He talked with Mrs. Priestly alone in her room and then he left. Mrs. Priestly told me not to tell anyone else in the family about the visit. She was trembling by then and pale, and I was afraid for her. And that night, she was killed by an intruder who climbed into her bedroom."

"Did the intruder take anything?"

"No. The police consensus is the killer didn't expect to find anyone in that room and panicked. She was killed with her pillow. I read in the paper that it appeared to be an impromptu killing because the weapon wasn't brought to the scene."

"But you said Mrs. Priestly kept her valuables nearby."

"Yeah, but out of sight, in a wall safe she often didn't lock."

"So, after her death, did anyone tell the investigating police about what Mrs. Priestly thought she witnessed?"

Obviously agitated, Cassie sat forward, hands waving as she spoke. "Yes, of course. They tore the backyard apart, but it had been raining for two or three days by then and they found nothing. *If* there was anything to find in the first place. That's what we don't know."

"And you don't think there was," he said.

"I didn't until I saw that article in the paper this morning."

He thought about the page he'd scanned. "You mean the drowning victim pulled out of the river?"

"It's been almost a week. It could be the man Mrs. Priestly said she saw killed."

"Or it could be someone else."

"I know, I know. It spooked me to see it. I guess I overreacted."

"Well, when we speak to Sheriff Inkwell, we'll tell him and let him do the follow-up—"

"No," she interrupted. "I don't want to talk to him."

He heard the resolve in her voice. "Cassie, I thought we agreed we'd tell the sheriff everything."

"And risk getting hauled back to Idaho? No thank you. No one followed us, no one knows who we are or where we live."

"What about your landlord? He probably thinks you were blown to bits."

"They won't find any part of me in that rubble."

"I don't think we want him worrying about you. He may have already talked to the police or—"

"Cody, I called and left him a message, okay?"

"When did you call him?"

"This morning. From a pay phone."

"You left the room?"

"Yes."

"But I told you—"

"Let's get something straight," she said firmly, and the look she cast him stopped him dead. "I'm your wife. I don't take orders. Just drop it, okay?"

He clamped his jaw shut but his mind was spinning at the realization that Cassie—who was ten years younger than he was and had always listened to and weighed his opinions—had apparently undergone some elemental changes.

Well, duh.

He was the one stuck in the past, trying to repeat old habits, relying on old feelings. If he wanted to stay married, he'd better figure out a way to win her trust back.

They passed a Jeep coming out of the gate as they drove under the Open Sky Ranch sign. A woman was behind the wheel and Cody exchanged a wave. "That's Doctor Wilcox from the university," he said, glad to have something less personal to talk about. "She's in charge of recovering the Native American remains at the cave. There's a big push now to get it done before the snow flies. I don't think they're going to make it."

"Isn't this kind of a roundabout way to get to the cave?"

"Very. They'd planned on using a different access but it didn't work out, so they park up here in one of the pastures and take ATVs out to the site."

They fell silent again as the road began the long descent into the valley where the ranch lay. He heard Cassie's sharp intake of breath as they crested the hill and the panoramic sight of the valley below presented itself.

The rolling fields, dotted with cattle—many were still in the high pastures and would need to be brought to lower elevations before bad weather set in. The spreading buildings with their brick-red roofs, including the log house he'd remodeled before bringing his bride home. The river that bisected the land, the glistening lake beyond, Adam's tall house sitting on the point near the lake, the fire damage of a few weeks before invisible from a distance. You couldn't see it from here, but Pierce had started construction on a home for himself and Princess Analise, situated on the other side of the lake.

Then there were the airfield and hangar, plus the numerous barns and outbuildings, the equipment used for harvesting and hauling, the trucks and tractors that kept the place up and running.

All familiar and loved.

And as always, to him, welcoming.

"It looks wonderful," Cassie said, her voice soft, the way he remembered. "I didn't allow myself to miss it before, but oh, Cody, it all looks like home." She reached over and put her hand on his leg. He glanced at her as he drove and saw her eyes were moist.

It *was* her home. *He* was her home. Things would be okay now. The land would remind her of their life; the land would remind them both of their beginning.

But she wouldn't be here now if someone hadn't tried to kill her.

Still, she was here. That was what mattered.

He was glad the ranch would be bustling with activity and family. The sheer number of people would help them bridge the uncomfortable moments of being back where they started.

A few minutes later, he drove into the yard. He'd never seen it so empty.

"Where is everyone?" Cassie asked. Her voice sounded half disappointed and half relieved.

"I'm not sure." Across the yard he saw Sassy Sally emerge from the barn carrying a bucket, Bonnie tagging along behind her, the stable hand, Mike, laughing by her side. Every time Cody saw Sally he shook his head at the incongruity of a statuesque Vegas showgirl giving up sequins and feathers for boots and jeans. She'd returned from vacation this year with an engagement ring and a fiancé who had moved to Woodwind to be closer to her, and she would soon be leaving the Open Sky for good.

The yellow Lab looked up first, saw Cody's truck and shot toward them like a greased pig.

"Bonnie!" Cassie called, as she slid out of the truck. The dog immediately veered toward her. Cassie did her best to kneel and the dog wiggled into her arms.

"She's shaking," Cassie said, looking up at Cody.

"She's just glad to see you."

Sally squealed as she approached. "Oh, my goodness, Cassie, look at you! You're going to have a baby any minute!"

Both women were tall blondes, although Cassie's hair was natural and Sally's came out of a bottle. Both were beautiful in their own way.

"Not any minute but soon," Cassie said, as Cody held out a hand to help her straighten up.

Mike, a big, friendly guy with a bushel of curly black hair and a penchant for working out, took the bucket from Sally. "I'll deliver the mash to Adam's horse. You stay and visit," he said, and loped off.

"Mike and I just got back from working on the gate over at Brandywine Gulch," she said. "It's a ghost town around here today with everyone at the Garvey trial."

"Isn't there a man named Garvey working here?" Cassie asked. "Lucas Garvey, right?"

"Lucas was killed last winter when he got mixed up in a kidnapping plot," Cody said. "This trial is for the oldest Garvey son, Hank. He went off the deep end a few months ago and tried to kill Adam."

"Wow," Cassie said, blinking.

Cody thought about all the things that had happened in the past few months, things she knew nothing about, things he would have to tell her.

But not all at once.

"Is Pierce home yet?" Cassie asked Sally. "And the princess?"

"Nope. They're still in Chatioux, but Adam mentioned they're returning next week. Everyone else went to the trial today, except Jamie and your uncle Pete are out working on the pump."

Cody was kind of glad no one else was home. This would give Cassie a chance to settle in. He grabbed his duffel out of the truck as Sally went back to work. Together, he and Cassie walked up the long walkway to the big front door. Bonnie stuck close to Cassie's side.

Cassie veered off the walk, her hand trailing along the railing as she moved toward the pond at the far end of the porch. He'd built it himself as a wedding present, and watching her stare into the quiet depths made him smile. Everything would work out. She was home now. The worst was over.

A few minutes later, they were upstairs. She emitted an audible gasp when she opened the door of what had always been their bedroom.

"You didn't change a thing," she said, walking around the green-and-yellow room, pausing to glance at their wedding photo on the wall: the two of them astride Cody's favorite gelding, Bandido, Cassie's white dress and veil billowing behind them in the breeze.

She touched it briefly, then turned to face him. "It feels like a time warp in here. I'll be honest—I'm surprised you kept it this way. I would have thought you'd have packed all my stuff away after a while."

"I never gave up hope I'd find you," he said, his voice gravelly.

"How could you stand to look at my things for all these months?"

"I couldn't," he admitted. "I slept down the hall."

Did that sound as pathetic to her as it did to him? He waited for her to add something—anything—but the silence between them was deafening and he didn't know how to break it.

She turned away and he took a steadying breath. When she glanced into the mirror over the vanity, their gazes met in the reflection, and for a second he hardly recognized her.

Suddenly he knew he couldn't stand another moment of being so close to her and yet so far away. Mumbling something about chores, he left in a hurry. Bonnie trotted out after him.

THE ROOM CLOSED IN ON Cassie after Cody left, and for one long moment she wished he'd never found her. She kept seeing his eyes in the reflection—if ever a man had looked trapped, he had.

Trapped. The very thing she'd been afraid of. The very reason she hadn't come home when she found out she was pregnant. It was all happening exactly as she'd anticipated.

Oh, yes, she knew he was glad she was here. There was a part of him that was obviously desperate to make things right, to rebuild the past. There wasn't a doubt in Cassie's mind that Cody had spent months reliving their last argument and blaming not only her but himself.

So he'd struggled to find her, and now the reality of what he'd found was hitting him in the middle of the face like a great big snow shovel.

And hitting her, too.

Because he was an honorable man, he would stand by her and their child forever. But if he retreated into himself the way his father had, what kind of life could they possibly have together? A wave of hopelessness drove her to sit on the edge of the bed, clutching her knees, head bowed, breathing deeply.

The baby delivered a few internal kicks, as though to put in his or her two cents. Something small and bony pressed back at her hands as she rubbed her skin, and she smiled and caught a sob at the same instant.

She had to get out of this room, away from this house.

A quick search of the closet revealed a green jumper she hadn't worn in a couple of years. She found a turtle neck that stretched over her midsection, then put on the jumper. It was a little snug but at least it was clean. She also found a pair of brown boots and tugged them on over kneesocks. A hasty search of the bottom drawer produced a big sweater, which she pulled on as she descended the stairs.

Once outside, she found the keys to the blue truck where they usually were—in the ignition. It was one of the ranch trucks and normally would be pressed into service toting fencing wire and tools hither and yon. With everyone at the Garvey trial or otherwise occupied, the truck was free for the taking and she took advantage of it, squeezing behind the wheel with some difficulty.

She chose the road to the airstrip with no goal in mind other than to be alone. She passed the hangar that housed the ranch Cessna, traveling toward the hills until she couldn't go any further. Then she parked the truck and got out. A path led uphill. The weather had deteriorated since she left the house, the clouds overhead darker and more dense. She wished she'd stopped to find a coat but knew the uphill climb would warm her up in a hurry. She tugged her blue scarf around her head and took off, wishing Bonnie was with her.

She'd given the dog to Cody for Christmas two years before. The ranch had always had dogs in the past, though there were none here now besides Bonnie, leastways, not as far as she knew. A Lab wasn't a herding dog, so it wasn't a work dog in this venue, and she knew Cody had been skeptical about her. But Bonnie had wormed her way into everyone's hearts, especially Cassie's. By the time Cassie left, she and Bonnie had become inseparable.

Who knew? Maybe she'd used the puppy as a surrogate child, pouring her love and nurturing into a dog because there was no baby.

Then. This was now. And Cassie could see Bonnie had transferred her loyalty to Cody. Just one more thing that had changed.

The path became increasingly steep and wooded, and she took a deep breath. As she walked, it was soothing to hear the crunch of the pine needles that covered a layer of last season's aspen leaves. There was a sense of homecoming out here the time-warp bedroom hadn't afforded. Soon there would be snow, and the world would become white and crisp.

Lots of distractions were in the offing. The holidays were coming, both Pierce and Adam were getting married, she was going to give birth.

And Cody, ready or not, was going to be a father.

Oh, and don't forget the possibility you'll wind up in jail.

There was a clearing up ahead, a spot on the edge of the hill that overlooked the lake. Farther up from that, a dirt road crisscrossed the land and provided access to a summer pasture.

The way was getting steep, but she'd spent most of her pregnancy pushing Mrs. Priestly's wheelchair on daily treks through the neighborhood, so she had no trouble with the paths. She walked beside a seasonal stream for a while, then veered off toward the clearing and the big rock upon which she would rest before starting the return trip.

From this vantage point she could see a new structure going up on the far side of the lake over near the path leading to the old hunting lodge. She sat down on the rock, which wasn't as easy as it used to be thanks to the baby, and discovered a stray shaft of light. She angled her face into its meager warmth and closed her eyes, letting her thoughts drift until she was in that warm, hazy place a mind enters when it's exhausted through and through.

She didn't want to think of poor Mrs. Priestly or the explosion in the apartment or the stolen jewels or the feeling of being hunted.

She didn't want to think of Robert Banner's grief over his grandmother's horrible death, or the look on Donna's face when she found out, or the way Emerson Banner's frosty gray eyes had shifted from person to person as the others cried.

Didn't want to think of the heartache that had made her run from this place and then stopped her from returning—all these things had spiraled together into this moment of time, and this moment of time was turning out to be quite tricky...

She rested her head on her folded arm and yawned. Sometime later, reality crashed its way into her consciousness when a pop in the air was followed by a searing pain in the arm that rested close to her stomach. Gasping, she pushed up the sleeve of her sweater to reveal blood oozing from torn flesh. Another pop and a sliver of rock by her shoulder whizzed into the air, hitting her cheek as it flew off.

Instinct rolled her the short distance to the ground even as her brain fought to accept the obvious.

Someone was shooting at her!

Chapter Six

Her knees absorbed much of the impact of the shallow fall. She lay still, hoping her assailant would think he'd fatally hit her and leave her to die.

What about the baby? How much jostling could a baby take?

Who was doing this? Who could be here? Why?

Was hunting season open? Was there a poacher on Open Sky land? Or maybe one of the students involved with the mine excavation had just shot at a squirrel.

A squirrel wearing a bright blue scarf?

Or had a person who had rigged an explosion in Cherrydell followed her here?

And then, heart jammed up in her throat, she detected the sound of someone coming down the hillside path. If she tried to get up and run she'd be shot in the back. She couldn't roll to safety because she was too pregnant. But she couldn't lie there like a bump on a log and wait for her attacker to finish the job, either.

Another noise reached her ears, this time from down the hill. It was like an invasion... She almost jumped out of her skin when a big, wet black nose pressed against her cheek. Bonnie! The dog looked over her head, up the hill, growled menacingly, then leaped up on the rock and beyond, barking like crazy. Cassie heard another shot and more crashing sounds. She tried to press herself into the earth and squeezed her eyes shut...

And jumped a half mile when a hand touched her head. A scream died in her throat as she twisted away and looked up—

It was Cody. He knelt beside her, touching her face. "Are you okay?" he whispered, withdrawing his hand. There was blood on his fingers.

"I—I think so. But Bonnie—"

"I'll be right back. Stay put."

Like she was going anywhere.

He took off up the hill, barely making a sound, while she worked on finding a better position so she could see what was going on. She felt light-headed as she gazed into the sky. The weather was turning, the clouds were heavy and dark. The baby kicked her—never had she been so glad to feel a healthy kick. She shivered with the cold.

The dog showed up first, once again nosing Cassie's skin, panting and excited. Cody arrived a minute or two later, barely out of breath. He pulled Bonnie away and helped Cassie sit up, her back against the rock.

She'd never seen his perpetually weathered skin that drained of color or his eyes that worried. "You're bleeding," he said, searching his pocket for the bandana he carried for emergencies. He wiped her face with it, then swore as he saw her arm. "We better get you to a doctor. Do you think you can stand?"

"I can stand. But where is the person who shot me? What happened? Is Bonnie okay?"

"Bonnie chased the shooter back up the hillside," he said, wrapping the bandana around her arm. She winced as he knotted the cloth to keep it in place. "Under all the blood, it looks like it's barely more than a scratch running along your skin," he assured her.

She'd started shaking, her teeth rattling together. A big plop of rain landed on her forehead. "I can't believe the gunman missed me *and* the dog."

Cody dug into his shirt pocket and extracted a couple of brass casings. "These are from a .380 autoloader, a pistol. I found them up on the road. Wrong gun for the occasion. No range."

"Did you get a look at a vehicle?"

"No. It was going around the bend by the time I got there. Bonnie probably saw it, but she isn't talking."

And then he did something that took her totally off guard. His hands landed softly, tenderly on her stomach. It was the first time he'd touched her that way since they reunited, and she jolted. He pulled away at once.

"It's okay," she murmured. Taking his hands, she placed them where he'd had them before. "Feel right there? That's a baby bottom or a head, I think."

He smiled as the baby rolled against his palms, then his eyes met hers. "If the bullet that grazed your arm had been a couple of inches further to the left—"

"I know. It could have been a tragedy."

He sat back on his heels, his hands gripped now between his knees. "So what in the hell were you doing up here by yourself?"

His question wasn't spoken loudly, but the anger that replaced the concern and tenderness of a moment before jolted her in a whole different way. "Wait a second—"

"Are you forgetting what happened in Cherrydell? And how did someone get to the ranch so fast? We've only been back a couple of hours."

"There was an emergency contact paper with your name on it in my purse," she admitted, as the cold rain picked up. "Someone must have seen it before you arrived, and then when you announced who you were, they put two and two together. We stopped last night at the inn, you know. They must have come straight out here and looked things over this morning."

He swore. "With all the increased coming and going because of the university, a stranger could go unnoticed. Why didn't you tell me someone had access to your true identity?"

She narrowed her eyes. "I just thought of it last night. I really didn't think it was very likely."

"Do you have any other little secrets that could end up getting you killed to say nothing of *my* baby?"

"*Your* baby? Since when is this *your* baby?"

"Since the moment my sperm said 'Howdy Ma'am' to your egg."

She glowered at him for a second.

He took a deep breath as he took off his hat and settled it on her head to protect her face from the rain.

"Okay, I'm sorry, Cass. This is a hell of a time for us to argue. If you can't walk I'll go down and get Bandido and bring him back for you."

"And leave me here alone? No way. I can walk."

Standing, he offered her a hand.

She accepted his help but still had to struggle. Getting on your feet, on a slope, while vastly pregnant wasn't exactly a piece of cake.

And neither was being shot.

WHEN CODY HAD LEFT Cassie in their bedroom, he'd needed some kind of outlet, and there just wasn't anything better for that than getting on a horse. He'd saddled up Bandido and ridden across the fields with a hazy goal of checking the nearby trail that they would take out to the Hayfork field when the time came to collect that part of the herd. He'd found the trail in good condition, and by the time he'd gotten back to the ranch he'd worked off a little of his anxiety.

And then he discovered Cassie and the blue truck were both missing.

His first thought: she'd taken off again. He'd wasted time kicking rocks and swearing. Then his head cleared and he somehow knew she wouldn't have done that without leaving so much as a note.

She had to be nearby, maybe as antsy as he'd been. And if she was still on the ranch and she'd used a vehicle, that probably meant she went to the airfield or Adam's place on the lake. With Adam at the trial, it seemed unlikely she'd go there.

She loved the trail by the hangar, but would she really hike uphill in her condition?

Of course she would. She'd walked with firm, fast steps the day before when he'd followed her. She was built like an athlete, slender but strong, and he doubted pregnancy had slowed her down much. So he'd taken off like a maniac, relieved when he found the blue truck parked at the foot of the trail. He'd tied Bandido to the truck and started up the trail with Bonnie at his side, climbing at a fast clip until he heard the first shot, and then he'd taken off at a dead run.

His first glimpse of her huddled down by that rock had frozen his heart midbeat. He'd thought for sure she was dead. If the marksman had been a better shot or chosen the right weapon, she would have been.

And if this gunman—or woman—was as persistent as it appeared, they'd try again…

Cody and Cassie arrived at the bottom of the path more wet than dry. The rain had taken on a slightly icy feel as the storm darkened the sky. They piled into the blue truck with Bandido trailing behind, tethered by a long rope to the gate of the truck, Bonnie in the bed.

"Are you sure you're okay?" he asked Cassie for the tenth time.

"I'm good. Really," she said. Taking a deep breath, she sat back in the seat, looking vulnerable in her wet clothes and his hat. Her delicate hand rested atop the bulge in her middle, the bandana still wrapped around her arm.

His heart just about exploded with the all the things he felt for her. As they started the trip back to the house, he wondered if she sometimes reeled with the same sense of convoluted déjà vu that he did. The last thirty-six hours had seen alternating episodes of the past colliding with the present. Riding in the truck? As ordinary as the rain. Explosions and gunfire? Surreal.

And he didn't have the slightest idea where they stood with each other except on rocky ground.

He needed a map of some kind. Some key to unlock what she was really feeling and what she wanted, because as a mind reader he suspected he was worse than most men except maybe his father.

That was probably why he'd always felt more comfortable with animals instead of people. Animals required things, sure, but they didn't have hidden agendas. They didn't play games.

It was one of the reasons he'd put off marriage so long, and had planned to put off fatherhood. Talk about needing to anticipate needs. And he was just lousy at that.

But it was too late. A baby was coming the way it seemed they always did—out of the blue. And today when he'd felt his son or daughter move inside Cassie's body, he'd felt the first strong stirring of connection.

"It looks like everyone is home," Cassie said, leaning forward to peer through the rain. Sure enough, the house was lit up inside and out, and figures could be seen moving across the yard.

"We'll go inside and call Inkwell—"

"I don't want to call the sheriff," she said.

"Come again?" She had to be kidding.

"The rain has undoubtedly washed away all traces of the vehicle from the dirt road," she continued. "What is Sheriff Inkwell going to do except demand to know why someone would want to hurt me and I can't even tell him that because I don't know but if I contact him he *will* find out that I'm wanted for questioning and he *will* turn me over and I *will* have to go back to Cherrydell and who knows what story the Banners will have and how long I'll be stuck there?"

She said it all in one breath, fast and furious. He wasn't any more anxious than she was to get involved with the law, but he wasn't convinced they had a choice. So much had gone on at the ranch this year that had brought in police that he wasn't anxious for repeats. Was it possible to keep Cassie safe?

"I just want to remind you that the someone who just winged you already knows who you are and where you live," he said.

"Just give me a few weeks," she pleaded. "Just let me have my baby."

"I'm not the one trying to stop you."

"I know. I just can't face going back to Idaho right now."

And he didn't want her to go back. "We'll have to agree to a plan," he said.

"What do you mean?"

"I mean we'll have to agree how to go about keeping you safe. No more wandering around by yourself, okay? I can stick around more than usual seeing as what time of year it is, and my father and brothers can take up the slack, but you'll have to be willing to stay low until this is figured out." He rubbed his wet head and looked over at her. "About a doctor—"

"I'm okay for tonight. The baby is moving around like crazy. Sassy Sally has EMT training. She can check out my blood pressure and all that, and tomorrow I'll find an obstetrician."

"Echo has training, too," Cody said. "But promise to tell me if anything goes wrong."

"Of course I'll tell you."

"Because when I saw the truck missing today the first thing I thought—"

"Was that I had run away?" she finished for him.

He nodded curtly. "Yeah."

"And how would you have felt about that? Kind of free? Kind of relieved?"

"That's a crummy thing to say, Cass."

She took off his hat and handed it to him. "I know it is. I'm sorry. But you can't go around waiting for me to leave again. I told you I wouldn't."

He took his hat from her. When he spoke, his voice was soft. "Let's just say I know why you're here and it's not because of me."

She stared at him and he knew he'd just blown it— again. "Cassie," he began, but at that moment, there was a knock on Cassie's window and her door opened.

Adam stood there, grinning. "Welcome home," he said. "Man, you two look like a couple of drowned rats. Sassy Sally told us about the baby," he added, his gaze darting down to Cassie's stomach. "That's great news." His gaze transferred to Cody. "Everything okay?"

"Not entirely," Cody said. "There was a shooting up on the hill. Cassie was hit."

"What!"

"I'm okay, really," Cassie said, lifting her arm as if to prove it.

"I'll explain in a while," Cody added.

Adam's gray eyes narrowed. He knew as well as Cody did that there'd been more violence connected to the Open Sky in the past six months than in the one hundred and twenty preceding years. "There's a big fire burning in the living room," Adam said, zeroing in on Cassie again. "Pauline is whipping up dinner, and you know she's a hell of a cook. Come on inside and get warm. We've all missed you."

Cassie patted her hair in a fruitless attempt to tidy it and fumbled with her seat belt. Cody could feel her apprehension and knew she wished she could avoid the next few minutes, but big families tended to be in and out of each other's lives and never more than when they all lived and worked together, breathing the same air, striving toward the same goals. And then around here you added the people who weren't family but as good as: the foreman, Jamie, and Pauline, the housekeeper.

The upside was that when one member stumbled, someone was always around to help them back to their feet.

"Come on, Cass," Adam urged, his voice soft. "I want you to meet Echo."

And that extra encouragement seemed to be enough, for the next thing Cody knew, Cassie had slipped out of the truck. She gave him a glance over her shoulder as she allowed Adam to lead her through the rain and into the house.

And suddenly Cody was as nervous as she was. He took off for the barn.

"Wow, THAT SCARF is gorgeous," Sassy Sally said as Cassie slipped the damp blue silk from around her neck.

"You think so?"

"Yes. It matches your eyes."

Cassie folded it into Sally's hands. "You know what? It matches your eyes, too. It's a little damp, but please, take it."

"But—"

"I bought it used. Now I'm finished with it. Please, I'd really like you to have it."

Sally accepted it and laid it aside. "Thanks. Ethan will love it."

"Is Ethan the new fiancé I've heard talk about?"

"Yeah. He's not as handsome as Cody—who is? But he's everything I've always wanted. He's sweet, he's kind, and he's a veterinarian to boot. He took a partnership in Woodwind to be close to me. I can't believe how lucky I am. I'm still pinching myself."

"I'm so happy for you," Cassie said, and she meant it.

"Cody told me what's been going on," Sally added, as she skillfully dressed Cassie's wounds. She took Cassie's blood pressure next, then listened with a stethoscope to Cassie's heart and the baby's. "You're in great shape, but I don't think it takes a medical degree to advise you to stay quiet for a few days. You're really pregnant, and all that falling and stuff can't be good. You'll speak up if you go into early labor or bleed or anything, right?"

"I'll scream like a banshee," Cassie assured her.

"Good." Sally returned the stethoscope and other supplies back to the ranch medical kit, then handed Cassie a piece of paper. "Cody asked if I know of a good obstetrician. This is the name of the guy who delivered my friend's baby last year."

"You guys about done in here?" Adam asked from the doorway. He looked a lot like Cody. A few years younger, coloring a little lighter, resembling their father more, but the same tall, square-shouldered cowboy frame, the same smile. Maybe it was just that his smiles came along more frequently than Cody's did.

And never more than now. Cassie noticed how often her brother-in-law's gaze settled on Echo, who had wandered into the room a few moments before him. She revealed she had taken accelerated EMT training at the university. With Sally leaving, Echo claimed, someone on the ranch needed basic medical knowledge.

Echo was about as opposite from the bleached, opulent Sally as a woman the same age could get. A television producer until falling in love with Adam, she sported a lithe figure, very short, glossy dark hair, remarkable black eyes and a quick, sassy wit. The smoldering way she and Adam looked at each other was a painful reminder to Cassie of what she and Cody had lost.

"Pauline says dinner's ready," Adam added. "Can you join us, Sally?"

"Not tonight," she said. "I'm driving into Woodwind to have dinner with Ethan. Bye everyone." She tossed the blue scarf around her neck and added, "Thanks again, Cassie."

Dressed in a dry jumper, Cassie went down to dinner, which was being served that night around the butcher-block island in the kitchen. Cassie thought she detected

Pauline's hand in that decision—it was much more intimate than the dining room.

Pauline stopped ladling soup into a tureen as she saw Cassie. They'd always been friendly with each other. Pauline rushed over for hugs, her round face wreathed in smiles.

"I am so happy you're back," she said. "And with a bun in the oven, too! What is it, a girl or a boy?"

"I don't know," Cassie said, looking around the country kitchen for a glimpse of Cody, but he wasn't there. "I didn't find out."

"I love a surprise," Pauline gushed. "A holiday baby! Is there anything better?"

"That goes for me, too," Birch said, and Cassie turned to her father-in-law, who was seated at the island. The last time she'd seen him his steel-gray hair had been longer, his complexion pale due to the broken knee and the subsequent infections that had plagued him all winter. He appeared much healthier now, his skin a better shade, the old snap back in his eyes.

"I was beginning to think I was never going to have another grandchild," Birch continued. "Pierce was so out of sorts after his son died, I thought he'd never find his way back. And Adam seemed content to wait for a girl to drop in his lap. We all thought he was nuts, but look what happened. Echo came—"

"—and more or less dropped in his lap," Echo finished with a laugh.

"And as for Cody, well, he shocked the hell out of me when he allowed himself to marry you. I just never thought he'd be able to take the next step and have himself a baby. Glad to see you talked some sense into him."

Birch's gaze met Cassie's and there was a question lurking in the depths, one she'd been expecting. She said, "Did Cody tell you why I left?" Her gaze took in the others. "Did he tell any of you?"

"Not exactly," Adam said.

"You tell us," Birch said.

She shook her head. "No, that's for him to explain in his own way." Curiosity burned in every set of eyes. They were all wondering why she'd stayed away practically her whole pregnancy if this was Cody's baby. Cody needed to sit everyone down and be frank with them, tell them the truth.

"Eat something, dear," Pauline urged. "You must be hungry. You're eating for two now, but you're skinnier than ever."

Cassie sat, painfully aware everyone was either staring at her or trying not to.

Adam brought up details of the trial and soon focus shifted away from Cassie. "I'm worried about Dennis Garvey," Adam said, as the back door blew open and Cody and Bonnie entered the adjoining mudroom. He was followed by an older man Cassie easily pegged as a Westin. Same bold features and rangy build.

Echo introduced her stepfather, Pete Westin, Birch's younger brother, to Cassie as Bonnie settled on her dog bed and Cody hung his wet hat on a hook.

"Why are you worried about Dennis?" Birch asked.

"I'm afraid he'll go down the same path his brothers went down," Adam said. "I don't think he's as intrinsically worthless as they are, however, but I don't know how to help."

"He's only what, sixteen?" Echo asked.

"Turns seventeen in a few weeks," Adam said. "I feel for the kid. Folks dead and surviving brothers both major losers. I mean, you can see Hank is going to go to jail for several years, and Tommy will face criminal charges once he heals. Dennis is pretty damn alone in the world."

Cody nodded. "It's a shame."

"Whole family is a waste of time," Birch said, as he poured himself hot coffee out of an insulated carafe. "We got our own problems. We need to bring back the herd still up at Hayfork pasture. This year I want them closer to the ranch before the weather turns. That field is just too far away. Then there's the Herefords over at Straw Creek. Soon as Pierce arrives, we need to go fetch them, too."

"What we need is someone who's good with a rope," Adam said. "I mean besides Pierce."

Cassie only half-listened to the conversations whirling around her. For her there was really only one other person in the room, and that was her husband. She loved it when he was like this: a little worn, a little frayed, a little tired—gorgeous. It was one of the times where his masculinity didn't confuse her at all, and it reminded her of the first time she'd seen him.

She'd gone to the rodeo with a wannabe cowboy, a guy named Josh who wore new jeans and pearl buttons on his stylized shirt. She'd been bored out of her mind.

Until they hit the bull-riding arena. And that was where her attention had been captivated by a tall, good-looking cowboy who shot out of the chute atop two thousand pounds of angry Brahma. He held on for a bloodcurdling eighty-eight seconds before being tossed in the air and falling to the ground. When he'd gotten to his feet and reclaimed his hat, his gaze had met hers. And as the brim had slowly settled above his dark eyes, she had known she'd just met her match.

He was staring at her now in the same intense way

he had at the rodeo. A shot of pure lust flooded her as he turned his attention to his brother and father.

"I spoke with Jamie and Mike out in the barn," Cody said, as Pauline delivered the tureen of vegetable beef soup and a basket of crusty bread to the island. "I've asked them to keep a sharp eye, especially when it comes to strangers."

"What's this about?" Birch demanded.

Cody placed both hands flat on the table. "Someone is trying to kill Cassie."

The comment hung there a second, then Cody perched on the stool next to Cassie. "Let me explain," he said.

She watched their faces as he spoke, expecting to see signs of shock or horror as the details unfolded, but she should have known better. It took a lot to rattle a Westin man or the kind of woman a Westin man was drawn to.

As Cody finished, Adam put down his spoon so hard it rattled against the bowl. "No one can get past all of us, Cassie. We've defended this place from worse things than a bad marksman. You'll be safe here."

Echo nodded in agreement.

But it was Pauline who heaved a deep sigh. "Lord have mercy," she murmured. "Here we go again."

Chapter Seven

Cody was relieved when Cassie, pleading fatigue, excused herself to go up to their room. After the difficult conversations of the afternoon, he didn't think he could take anymore. By the time he was ready to retire, though, he was sorry they hadn't discussed sleeping arrangements.

Should he move back in with her tonight or wait until tomorrow? Was she laying there wondering where he was, or was she relieved she didn't have to put up with him? How could she have been back for most of a day without them figuring out where they were going to sleep?

You left, remember? he reminded himself. *You got all uncomfortable and ran away to the barn and the horses where you felt safe, so don't blame her.*

Leaving Bonnie on her blanket downstairs, he entered the small room he'd been using since March, but it seemed a mile away from Cassie. What if the killer decided to close in at night? If this was the same person who had murdered Mrs. Priestly, they'd proven they knew how to break into a second-story bedroom. There were ladders all over this ranch, and the gunman had obviously looked around while the place had been more or less deserted. Otherwise he never would have known he could advance on Cassie from that particular road.

Cody paced a little. He needed a shower and dry clothes and a decent night's sleep so he could function. He accomplished the first two, redressing in jeans just in case he needed to be ready to defend Cassie from some new disaster, and dug through his duffel for the book he couldn't seem to get into. Maybe tonight he could finally concentrate.

But the book wasn't there. Maybe Cassie had stuck it in her purse in their rushed haste to leave the inn.

What he did find was the small black box containing the ring he'd intended to give her to cement their new beginning. Somehow, what they had so far still didn't feel like much of a beginning. Sticking the box in his robe pocket, he went downstairs and into the office. A painting of the old hunting lodge hung behind the desk. He moved it aside to get to the safe located in the wall beneath, opened it and deposited the box.

Then he climbed the stairs again and strode down the hall like he was getting ready to rope a steer, nerves flaring in his gut. He was going to sleep in his own room. It was safer for Cassie. That was his reasoning, or at least the part of his reasoning he was comfortable thinking about.

He opened the bedroom door as quietly as possible. Cassie lay asleep on her side of the bed. She'd left the lamp on his side burning, which he took as a good sign. But in the end, he couldn't bring himself to join her. Instead he settled with a blanket in the upholstered armchair, turning it to face the window.

He listened to her breath, listened to the rain against the window, listened to his own heart beating and yawned.

He awoke when hands touched his. Cassie leaned over him, her loose blond hair falling forward in a fragrant cloud of honey gold. She looked like an angel.

"Come to bed," she whispered, tugging on him. He got to his feet, stripped off everything but his underwear, and made it into bed, where he scooted close to her and opened his arms. She curled against him, her head right beneath his nose, just as she always had.

He wanted her in the worst way possible.

It seemed forever since they'd made love, and now didn't seem a real good time to enter into a discussion of the merits of sex during the late stages of pregnancy. He settled for kissing her hair and running his fingers over her petal-soft skin until one hand drifted to rest atop the baby. He could feel no movement and for a while that worried him, and then there was a tiny push beneath his fingers. Reassured but exhausted, Cody drifted into dreamless slumber.

The next morning, waking in their room, dressing within sight of each other, Cody finally felt as if he was married again. He was fascinated with the changes in Cassie's body. Besides the obvious bulge in the middle, her breasts were fuller, too. She was simply bursting with sexy new curves her nonmaternity wardrobe couldn't disguise.

"You're staring at me," she said, as she loosely braided her hair.

"I've always loved watching you dress, you know that," he said, pulling on his boots.

She came around to his side of the bed and perched on the mattress in front of him. "I don't look the same as I always looked," she said.

"No, you're even prettier."

"Bigger, anyway."

He got off the chair and sat down next to her. Placing his open hand on her rounded jaw, he stroked her skin, and she leaned against him. Her soft hair teased the back of his hand. Her earlobe was like a drop of satin against his fingertips. He kissed her cheek and heard her sigh, and then he kissed her lips.

How could a moment be so tender and so explosive at the same time? It was, though, and he knew her well enough to know it was the same for her. He'd felt that quickening response before, and it drove him insane. He kissed her deeper as he pulled her against him, and there was no hesitation in her response.

"Oh, Cassie," he said against her skin, as he trailed kisses down her neck.

"I know, I know," she said, cupping his chin and raising his head to look into his eyes. "I was beginning to think we'd never—"

"I know," he said, nuzzling her neck again.

"Why didn't you come to bed last night? Why did you sit in that chair?"

Her question caught him off guard. "I was worried about you."

She withdrew, not in distance, but in attitude. He could feel it, like clouds covering the sun. She finally whispered, "Did you think I was going to sneak off in the middle of the night?"

"No," he said, startled. "I was afraid someone might try to climb in the window!"

She closed her eyes for a second. "Oh."

"I wasn't—"

Her eyelids fluttered open and she covered his lips with her fingers. "I made a mistake. I jumped to a conclusion."

He kissed her fingers. "It's okay—"

"No, it's an indication of how we need to take it slowly and figure this all out."

"Our original plan."

"Yes. If we skip building something we can both trust, there will always be misgivings. You'll be thinking I'll leave when the danger is past. I'll be thinking you're waiting for me to go because I've tricked you into a child you weren't ready for."

"That again," he said, but he could also sense the wisdom of her words even though he didn't want to hear them. He stood up and looked down at her. "First things first," he said.

"Yes. And one of the first things you need to do is talk to your dad and brothers. I'll do it with you, if you want, but they have to understand what really happened between us or they're going to wonder if I got pregnant after I left here. In other words, they're going to wonder if this baby is really yours."

"Yeah, I can see that. I'll talk to them this morning."

"Thank you."

Back to being formal. "By the way, did you pack my book when we left the inn? It's one I borrowed from Uncle Pete."

"No."

"And about a doctor—"

She looked away from him. "I don't know."

"Cassie? Come on. Be reasonable. Please. You need to have a new doctor."

"Okay, okay, I'll call," she said, struggling to get to her feet. He gave her a helping hand. Cradling the bump, she added, "Does it seem to you I'm getting bigger by the second?"

He smiled, and because he couldn't help himself, leaned down and briefly kissed her lips.

An hour later, she'd made an appointment with the doctor who'd had a timely cancellation, and by late afternoon they were back on the road, driving toward Woodwind.

Cody had spent the first part of the day working on chores with the other men, as his father and Uncle Pete had forgone the dubious pleasure of accompanying Adam and Echo to court. He knew Cassie had spent the morning helping Pauline bake, and he wondered if she'd really enjoyed it or if she missed being on her own. They drove to Woodwind in near silence, but it wasn't oppressive, just thoughtful. At least he hoped that was all it was.

An hour later he realized why Cassie had seemed jittery about coming in to see the doctor.

"You've never even had an ultrasound?" Dr. Falstaff asked after the initial examination. "Or a blood test or anything?" He was a man of fifty with a halo of graying frizz and lively blue eyes, kind of like a thin, new age version of Santa Claus.

Cassie shook her head. "I went to a clinic when I could, you know for prenatal vitamins and such. They had connections with a midwife. I was planning on using her. My pregnancy has been uneventful until the last couple of days and even then, I've no twinges or indications anything is wrong. It's just that now that I'm not near the midwife, I decided I should get to know a doctor."

He settled back in his chair. "Well, we'll run your blood tests and order an ultrasound if there are any problems, but it seems to me you're doing well. I wouldn't be surprised if the baby comes early, though," he added, as he cleaned and redressed Cassie's gunshot wound. "Take it easy for the next few weeks, okay? No more jumping around, and stay away from people who don't know how to handle a gun."

"The stable hand didn't mean to hurt me," she said, as the doctor treated the scratch on her face, too. Cody sat by, amazed, as she rattled off this fictional tale of an inept stable hand when Falstaff recognized the gash for what it was. He was doubly amazed that she hadn't seen a doctor until now. She was just full of surprises.

"He was cleaning the gun and it discharged," she added.

The doctor shook his head. "Still, do us all a favor and stay away from him."

She met Cody's gaze and he saw the memory of being shot at blaze in her eyes. "Oh, I plan to," she said. "You can count on it."

THEY MADE A QUICK STOP at a department store so Cassie could replace some of the maternity basics she'd lost in the explosion. While she tried things on, Cody wandered off, so after she'd paid for her choices she had to go look for him. In the past, he had usually wound up in the tool section or perusing the books, so she walked right past the baby aisles until she caught a glance of his brown Stetson.

There he was, all six feet two inches of him, considering a pink-and-blue receiving blanket, then a green-and-yellow. Then she noticed he also had a cart nearby, and it was piled high with everything from diapers to booties. There was a car seat, too, and a box of rattles.

For a second, her vision blurred. Never in a million years had she thought she'd find Cody Westin addressing the merits of baby blankets, or any other infant accessory for that matter.

A saleswoman bustled up to him, speaking as she

moved. "I found the music mobile you asked for, sir. It's up at the desk when you're ready."

He murmured his thanks as she left, then noticed Cassie. "Which blanket do you like?" he asked, a shy smile hovering in his eyes.

"The green-and-yellow."

That one went into the basket, the other one got folded rather ineptly and replaced on the shelf.

She looked at him closely, trying to reconcile this Cody with the Cody she'd known for the past four years. No way.

"You don't have to keep these things if you don't like them," he said, misreading her speculative stare. He tapped the biggest box and added, "The salesgirl said this is the highest-rated car seat, though, and we have to have one of them, right?"

"Everything is perfect," she said, kind of over-whelmed with it all.

After they'd carried everything to the truck, Cody announced he wanted to stop by the inn, which was just across the street, to see if they'd found his uncle's book. He looked surprised when she got out of the truck to accompany him into the office, but she'd made a decision back at the department store when she'd watched him shop.

If they were going to rebuild a married life better than the one they had before, then they needed to start acting married. Doing things together. Sharing things. Little things as well as big things. They had less than a month to make a stable family for their baby—time was a'wasting.

And so, face it, was honesty. She would tell him about the jewelry she'd discovered in her handbag and sent back to the Banners. No more secrets. She got out of the truck and made her way around to his side. When she took his hand, he repaid her with a soft kiss on her cheek.

Inside the office, they found a thirtyish woman behind a desk. She asked if they needed a room. Cody told her his name and explained where he'd left his book the night before last.

"One of the maids turned it in yesterday, Mr. Westin," she said, as she slid open a drawer. "In fact, I called your home a little while ago and talked to a woman named Pauline to tell you that we'd found it." As she handed him the book she added, "Did you run into your cousin yet?"

"My cousin?" he asked.

"A kind of average-size gal with red hair. She didn't leave her name. She said she was supposed to meet you and your wife but she got held up."

"When was she here?" he asked. His voice sounded suspicious. There were no Westin cousins besides Echo, and she was a cousin only by virtue of Cody's uncle Pete marrying her mother.

"A couple of hours ago. I told her you'd left yesterday."

"Did you mention where we live?"

"I think it came up," she admitted, as her gaze swept over Cassie's blossoming figure. "I mean, she was your family and knew all about your baby and everything. A group of guests seeking restaurant information came in about then and I lost track of her. You haven't met up with her yet?"

"Not yet," Cody said.

As they left the office, Cassie braced herself for what was sure to come next, holding her breath until Cody had helped her back into the truck, then climbed behind the wheel.

"Who's looking for you now?" he said, turning to face her. His voice was calm but his eyes were darker than thunderclouds.

"It sounds like Donna Banner Cooke."

"Any idea how she could have known where we stayed—unless she followed us?"

Cassie gently rubbed her forehead. Donna's presence in Woodwind cast a deep shadow on the aura of normalcy that had been burning bright that day. Until now.

"I don't get this," Cody added. "Someone shoots at you yesterday, which makes it clear they knew exactly where you live, then asks questions about your whereabouts today? It doesn't make sense."

"I don't get it, either," she said.

"I have to tell you, from where I'm sitting, your identity seems to be the worst-kept secret in Wyoming."

"Yeah? Well, there's something you *don't* know about."

His eyes narrowed as he stared at her. "Why aren't I surprised to hear that?"

"Listen, Cody Westin, don't get snotty with me. We really haven't had a decent conversation since we got back together. There are bound to be things—"

"Like the fact you didn't have a regular doctor?"

"I went to a clinic! It's hard to see the kind of doctor you're talking about when you don't have insurance."

"You had insurance."

"But I didn't have an identity."

A knot bulged in his jaw, but at least he didn't counter with the fact that she knew perfectly well she had an identity, and all she had to do was claim it. Instead he said, "You're talking about things that happened before you left Idaho."

She bit her lip. "Well, of course. But even other things…"

"I don't like the sound of that."

"I'm not thrilled with it either, trust me," she said. "But you have to know. I should have told you sooner."

He cleared his throat in a way she knew meant he was struggling with patience. "You're scaring the daylights out of me," he said after a pause. "What are you talking about?"

"I think I know how Donna found out about the inn. After we left Cherrydell I found a bunch of jewelry sewn into my purse the same way it had been sewn into the lining of my suitcase back at the Priestly house. I'm not sure why I didn't just tell you."

She saw his gaze shift and she took a deep breath. "Okay, you're right, I do know. You would have insisted we take it to the sheriff and I didn't want to do that, so I mailed the items back to the Banners yesterday. That put a Woodwind postmark on the envelope, and I used a washcloth to pad everything. I didn't think to check— the name of the inn must have been on the washcloth label or something like that. I never dreamed they would come looking for me."

"That's why you left when I went to get breakfast. To mail a package of jewels."

"And make the phone calls, yes."

He sat there staring at her.

"Come on, Cody," she said with a gentle pat on his thigh. "Start the truck. We'd better get back to the ranch and see what Donna wants."

He did as she asked, but the relaxed silence of the

drive into town was gone, replaced by retreats to their own corners.

"I know you're angry with me," she said, when they entered Open Sky land.

He cast her a swift glance. "I don't know if I'm angry or just terrified of your recklessness."

"I've turned over a new leaf," she said.

"I hope so. But this isn't all your fault. You're right about us not talking. I haven't wanted to say the wrong thing so I've been saying damn near nothing."

"I know."

"That can't go on."

"You're right."

"So let's make a new deal. No more secrets. And from now on we make important decisions together."

"Okay," she said, amazed that they'd arrived at the same place today by such different paths. As they pulled into the yard they found a long black vehicle with Idaho plates parked by the front walkway.

"Is that Donna's car?" Cody asked.

Cassie narrowed her brow as she thought. "You know, I don't think I ever saw her car, but the plates are a dead giveaway, right?"

At that moment, the driver's door of the sedan opened and a man in a black suit with a dark overcoat got out.

Cassie covered her mouth as she gasped. Emerson Banner stood there in the waning light, scrutinizing their advancing truck as though thinking of ways to blow it up. Funny that should be the image that came to her.

His icy gaze cut through the windshield, and she flinched.

Chapter Eight

"What in the hell is he doing here?" Cody said.

He hadn't liked the man the first time he'd set eyes on him, and he didn't like him now. And he really didn't like being ambushed on his own land. He regretted sending Bonnie off with his father to mend fence. It would be kind of nice to have the dog standing there barking at this yahoo.

"There's only one way to find out," Cassie said. Cody watched as she unbuckled her seat belt with trembling fingers. He took her hand in an effort to lend moral support, hating Banner even more when he noticed the derisive way he looked at Cassie.

He had cold, gray eyes, the kind that seemed to reflect light as though nothing got through them either coming or going. Today he seemed a little more fidgety than he had before, jumpy maybe, his hands jammed in his overcoat pockets, looking around as though expecting a herd of cows to stampede.

"This is quite a little spread you have here," Banner said.

Cody narrowed his eyes. "Well, it's not the first time you've seen it, is it?"

"Of course it is. What do you mean?"

"I mean you were here yesterday taking potshots at my wife," Cody said.

Banner managed to look startled. "I did nothing of the sort—although by all rights, I should have brought the police with me today."

"Why didn't you?" Cassie asked.

"Donna wouldn't allow it. She said you must have made a mistake."

"A mistake?"

"A mistake of omission," he said with a sneer. "But you and I both know what you made was a choice, not a mistake."

Cassie had stopped dead in her tracks. "I don't know what you mean," she said.

"I've come for what's mine. For what's Donna's."

"And what would that be?" Cassie asked.

"I'm not going to play games with you people," he said, glancing from one to the other. He took a step toward Cassie, which Cody intercepted.

"Maybe we're the ones who need to call the police," Cody said, as he stared down at Banner. "They might be interested in knowing if you own a handgun."

"Someone stole mine," Banner said. "It was a good one, too. I had it fitted with ivory grips, just like General Patton. Anyway, this is the West. Everyone owns a handgun."

"That's not true, I don't," a woman said, as she came along the deck from the direction of the pond. Despite her auburn hair, Cody could see the Banner family resemblance in her eyes and chin.

"Perhaps, Donna, but your husband has half a dozen," Banner said, scowling. "He's always shooting at things."

"I wish you wouldn't talk about Kevin that way," Donna said, and immediately turned her attention to

Cassie. "Laura," she said warmly. "It's so nice to see you."

Even though Cody knew Cassie had used her dead mother's name, this was the first time he'd seen her respond to it and it jarred him. Cassie stepped forward to be engulfed in a big hug.

"It's nice to see you, too, Donna, but what are you doing here? Have they found out who killed your grandmother?"

Donna took Cassie's hands in hers as tears filled her eyes. "No, no, still no idea. They keep asking me where Kevin is. If I knew where he was, I'd go get him. All I know is he didn't have a thing to do with Grandma's death."

"How do you know that?" Cassie asked.

Donna touched her chest. "Kevin would never harm anyone," she said with utter conviction.

"But he did disappear right after her murder," Cassie said gently.

"They have no leads or anything?" Cody asked.

Donna looked up at him as though noticing him for the first time. "They found a shoe print under Grandma's window right after her death, and yesterday they found a ladder with the same mud on it. It was in the neighbor's boathouse. He says he hasn't been in the building for months."

"The police are incompetent," Banner snarled.

"But why are you and your father here?" Cassie persisted. "I don't understand."

Donna lowered her voice. "Honey, I know you were desperate," she said. At the change in her demeanor, Cassie withdrew her hand from the other woman's clasp and clutched the collar of her coat closer to her chin. "Robert said I shouldn't blame you for taking Grandma's things. He said you were desperate and didn't have any money. But this ranch is beautiful. What were you doing at Grandma's house using a different name and everything? I don't get it."

"It's a long story," Cassie said with an upward sweep of her lashes toward Cody. "Let's just say I was confused. I'm home now."

"Well, that's good. I'm happy for you, I really am, although I kind of hoped you and Robert might hit it off."

"Over my dead body," Emerson Banner muttered.

"Mine, too," Cody said. At last, he and Banner had something they could agree on.

"Anyway," Donna continued, "I'm so glad you gave back the things you took."

"But how did anyone know they even came from me?"

"Who else?" Donna asked, wide-eyed. "You'd been caught before, and the postmark was Wyoming and your husband told Dad you were from Wyoming—it didn't take a brain scientist to put it together. Mom and Dad got the package in the morning mail, and then Dad called me and we decided to come after the last piece."

"What last piece?"

"Grandma's ring. You know, the emerald one? You sent the rest of the stuff, but you must have forgotten the ring. It was her favorite and it would mean the world to me to get it back."

"But I did return it," Cassie said. "It was in with the other things, sewn into the lining of my handbag."

"There, see, she admits she's a thief," Emerson Banner said, taking out his cell phone.

Donna turned to her father. "Dad, please, just wait a second." Addressing Cassie again, she added, "You sent the sapphire necklace and the ruby broach, but not the ring."

Cassie looked over her shoulder at Cody. "I did send it back," she said.

"Is it possible it fell out of the washcloth before you put everything in the envelope?" he asked, swearing at himself for indulging any of this. They should call the police and their lawyer right that second. He wouldn't put it past Banner to be carrying the gun he'd used to take shots at Cassie.

"I bet that's what happened," Donna said, and actually looked as though she believed it.

"Well if it did fall out it would be in my purse—"

Banner thrust a pointed finger at Cassie. "I knew it. After what you tried to get away with using your suitcase, I should have insisted we search everything you carried or wore." He looked at her shoulder bag. "Empty that thing right now."

"Back off," Cody warned.

"No, it's okay," Cassie said, as she slid Emerson Banner a nervous glance. "Please, come inside. Both of you."

"Wait just a second," Cody said. "Cassie, I don't think you should say another word without a lawyer." He looked from father to daughter and added, "Are you people pressing charges of some kind?"

Donna said, "No."

Banner said, "Yes."

"If the ring didn't arrive in the mail, then it has to be in my purse," Cassie insisted. "I want the opportunity to clear this up. I have not been stealing jewels. They've been planted on me, either to make me look guilty or to get them out of the house so they could be stolen back without anyone knowing. So, please, everyone calm down and come this way."

Cody followed along behind the three of them, watchful and alert. At the first sign of trouble, Donna and her father were getting the boot.

Cassie led the way into the living room, where a small fire burned in the grate. As Banner and Donna watched, Cassie upended her purse on the big, square coffee table, her possessions skittering here and there.

She methodically began separating things, going so far as to open her cosmetic bag and her wallet and shaking out the contents. She flipped through a notepad and a paperback book, the pages fluttering by without incident. She unrolled an extra pair of socks and patted them flat, unscrewed the lid on a small antacid bottle and emptied the contents into her palm.

"What about zippered pockets?" Emerson Banner demanded.

Cody swallowed a jab of anger. He was doing his level best to let Cassie handle these people as she'd made it obvious that was what she wanted. Him? He just wanted to kick the guy.

He heard a vehicle outside and he wondered if his brother and Echo were stopping by the ranch after a day in court, or if his dad was about to storm into the house and make things worse....

"Dad, please," Donna said, pulling on his arm. "Let's go. With Kevin gone, I need to get back to the shop."

"Just a moment," Cassie insisted, a bright spot of pink dotting each of her cheeks. "I have nothing to hide." She turned the leather satchel inside out and showed them the ripped seam, explaining she'd found the jewels the night she left Cherrydell and mailed them back the very next day.

"I wonder what happened to the ring," Donna said, staring at Cassie's pile of odds and ends.

Banner, who had sat on the sofa to be closer to the contents of Cassie's purse, shot to his feet, hands curled into balls, eyes brimming with venom. "This doesn't prove a thing," he said, once again taking out his cell phone. "She's had a day or two to hide things wherever she wanted. No, don't tell me to quiet down, Donna, this charade has gone on long enough. This woman is an opportunistic fraud. Don't forget she conned your grandmother into leaving her *your* inheritance, which means you'll get less and that husband of yours won't have as much to squander on that business of his. Even if the police don't consider her a murder suspect, she's proven herself a world-class liar and a thief, and I've heard enough."

"That's it," Cody said. He glanced at Cassie and added, "I'm sorry, honey, but this is too much. You can't expect me to stand here and listen to this. I'm going to call the sheriff. If this guy didn't shoot you yesterday, I'll eat my damn hat."

"How dare you try to blame some drummed-up blunder on me? As for your sheriff, what is he? Some hick you have sewn up in your back pocket. I know how that works, Westin. No thanks, I'll summon a real lawman."

From the direction of the dining room came a new voice, one low and soothing in its own rumbling way. "Now, I can't say as I much appreciate that kind of talk, Mr. Banner. Almost sounds like you're casting aspersions on the sheriff department."

Cody whipped around to find Sheriff Clayton Inkwell standing by the dining room table.

And he wasn't alone.

As Cody watched, the sheriff, wearing his habitually

rumpled green jacket and a billed hat obscuring a thatch of gray-blond hair, sauntered into the living room followed by a younger, neater-looking officer dressed in a blue uniform. The closer he got, the more visible became the legend on the star-shaped badge on his chest.

He was from Idaho.

Cody tensed. Cassie, meanwhile, grabbed his hand. It was obvious she'd leapt to the same conclusion Cody had: the gig was up. She would be returned to Cherrydell for questioning.

"Cody, Mrs. Westin, nice to see you both," Inkwell said.

Cody shook Inkwell's proffered hand. "Nice to see you, too, Sheriff." He caught a glimpse of Pauline hovering behind the sheriff. She must have admitted the police through the kitchen door.

"How do you know my name?" Banner demanded, his gaze darting to the sheriff's silent partner, brow furling as he studied the man's badge. His frown immediately turned to a smile. "Ned Tucker? Are you Charlie's boy?"

"You know my dad?" the Idaho officer asked.

"You bet I do. We both belong to the same club. What in the world are you doing here?"

"Is it Kevin?" Donna asked, pushing her father out of her way. "Did you find my husband?"

"No, ma'am," the deputy said. "I mean, I don't know anything about your husband." The deputy was a solid-looking guy in his early twenties with a square torso and an even squarer jaw. "I'm here for you, sir," he added, looking at Banner. "Your wife told us where to find you. I'm real sorry, but I have a warrant. Seeing as we're in Wyoming, Sheriff Inkwell will make the arrest and then we'll extradite you to Idaho. You'll need to come with us."

Banner blinked rapidly as though reviewing past events behind his eyelids. "You have a warrant for *me?* That's crazy." He pointed at Cassie. "This woman is the thief."

As Cassie recoiled, the sheriff stepped in. "Now, hold on. You're in enough trouble as it is. The deputy has been telling me all about some mighty sad goings-on back there in Cherrydell." He rattled off the Miranda warning and cuffed Banner.

Banner turned his attention back to the deputy. "You don't honestly think I am guilty of any of that, do you now, Ned? This is all just a misunderstanding."

"I'm sure you'll get it cleared up real soon," Tucker said. "Meanwhile, I have to enforce the law. Ma'am," he added with a nod at Cassie's bulging midsection, "are you the woman who passed herself off as Laura Green?"

"Yes," Cassie said, shrinking back.

"You need to come back to Cherrydell and answer a few questions."

"Come on now, Deputy Tucker, just look at the lady," Inkwell said. "Mrs. Westin is in no condition to be driving over mountain roads. Mr. Banner is going to be our guest tonight anyway. How about these nice folks just come on down to my office and you can ask them anything you want, say, tomorrow morning?"

"There's lots of people have questions for her," the deputy said. "Mrs. Banner is thinking of pressing charges."

"Tomorrow morning," the sheriff said, his voice a hair more firm.

"I guess that would work," the deputy said. "I'll have to check."

Banner erupted again. "What do you mean I'm going to be your guest? I insist on going back to Cherrydell immediately."

Sheriff Inkwell chuckled. "See, this is how it goes. We have to do things a certain way and you have to live with it. Life is compromise."

Cody fought not to smile at Banner's predicament and Inkwell's folksy stubbornness. And despite Cassie's obvious concern at being thrown into the middle of that which she'd tried so hard to avoid, Cody was relieved everything was finally out in the open. He didn't much like secrets, especially when they threatened the life of his woman and unborn child. Sooner this all got cleared up, the better.

It didn't hurt that Emerson Banner was on his way to jail. That was just icing on the cake.

"What are you arresting me for?" Banner demanded.

"Well now, I can't speak for Deputy Tucker, but I just sort of assumed you knew," Inkwell said.

"Misappropriation of funds. For now," the deputy added.

"What's that mean?" This came from Donna, whose rosy complexion had paled to ash. "Dad, is he talking about embezzling from Grandma?"

Banner shook his head.

Donna sucked in air. "Robert said you were stealing, but I said, 'No, Dad wouldn't do that!' I've been a fool to defend you, haven't I?"

"Donna, for heaven's sake, pull yourself together," Banner snapped. "Call Gibbons. Have him meet me in Woodwind."

She look at the deputy and added, "What do you mean, that's all you're arresting him for *now?* What else is there?"

The deputy cast an apologetic look at Emerson Banner. "I'm sure this is all just a mistake," he said.

"Cody, how about you and Cassie come on down to the station in the morning," the sheriff added.

Cody glanced at Cassie. He wouldn't mention the explosion, because that happened in Idaho, but he'd be damned if he wouldn't bring up yesterday. "We'll be there. Meanwhile, you should know someone shot Cassie up on the hill above the lake when we got home yesterday. Winged her arm. My money is on Mr. Banner there. I'll bring in the spent casings."

"I told you, my revolver was stolen—"

"Did you report it?" the deputy asked.

"Not yet. I am now."

They all headed for the kitchen. Pauline, who was still hovering, hurried to get out of their way.

But Banner paused and looked over his shoulder, right at Cassie. "This isn't over, Mrs. Westin. My lawyer will make sure that you never get a single penny, and if there's any way on earth to prove you aided her killer, I won't rest until you pay."

The sheriff bundled him through the door.

Donna looked at Cassie, eyes wide. "Did you have something to do with my grandma's death?"

"Of course she didn't," Cody said. He'd had enough of all these people. His urge was to saddle up Bandido, lift Cassie on behind him and head for the mountains....

Sure. She could give birth in the snow. Great plan. His goal was keep her safe, not freeze her to death.

"Donna, your father is right," Cassie said, gripping the other woman's shoulders. "Get in touch with his lawyer. Call your mother and Robert."

"Okay," she said vaguely, as she started for the front door.

"Are you all right to drive?" Cody asked.

Donna paused. "Yeah. Shocked, you know, that's all. And Laura," she added, covering her lips and shaking her head. "I mean Cassie. Please try to find my ring. I've been wrong about everyone else. Don't make me regret trusting you, too."

As the door closed behind her, Cassie looked around the room like a caged animal, her gaze darting from the door to the windows to the rock fireplace, as though she were wishing she could turn herself into a wisp of smoke, drift up the chimney and float away on the wind.

She'd always been a rock, so sure of herself it spooked him. Seeing her like this made his gut itch. He caught her hand, and she turned to stare into his eyes.

"Now what?" she said.

He tugged her toward him, the baby bumping against his stomach first. His baby.

"Now we get through it together," he said. "All three of us."

Chapter Nine

The pregnancy made sleeping difficult. Hard to find a comfortable position that supported her ponderous middle, hard to stretch out when she was afraid of waking Cody, hard to stop thinking.

That was the real problem. Random thoughts skittered around in Cassie's head like startled ants. What had Deputy Tucker meant when he said that was all they were arresting Emerson Banner for *now?* Were there more charges in the offing? Did they suspect him of murdering Mrs. Priestly?

Was that why he was hurling accusations and threats at her—to take the attention off of himself? Had he gone so far as trying to blow up a pregnant woman or gun her down in her sleep?

And could anyone prove anything against him? If he'd been stealing from Mrs. Priestly, there must be some kind of tangible money trail, right? He couldn't schmooze his way out of that….

She got out of bed, stepped into her slippers and robe, and left the bedroom as quietly as she could, making her way down the stairs carefully. Slinking through the large, dark house in the middle of the night reminded her of the night less than two weeks before when she'd gone to check out what Mrs. Priestly claimed she saw through her bedroom window.

A murder. By the river. And that reminded Cassie of that article she'd seen in the paper about the body recovered downstream from Cherrydell. She'd all but forgotten about it until now, and she vowed to find out in the morning if the police had identified the man yet.

She walked through the dark house with the encouraging sensation of being home, of belonging. Bonnie greeted her in the kitchen, nuzzling against her legs, her eyes sleepy looking. But when Cassie opened the outside door and flipped on the electricity, the dog tore off into the night on some secret mission.

More memories of that night. The light hadn't worked. Well, it hadn't worked many times before that, either. The mansion was old. Cassie had overheard a couple of conversations where Emerson and Victoria had tried to coax Mrs. Priestly into spending money on upkeep, but the old woman hadn't seen the decay. Maybe her memories were more vivid than the present.

It had stopped raining, but it was cold. As Cassie stepped outside, she drew her robe as close as possible and moseyed around the deck, pausing when she got to the pond, loving the darkness, loving the quiet and, most of all, loving the thought of Emerson Banner behind bars.

She sat on the bench carefully, rubbing her stomach as she so often did now, and leaned back just a little to give the baby room. "No offense, but you are going to be a bruiser," she whispered, as she stared at the reflected moonlight in the pond that Cody had built for her.

How she had missed this pond. Oh, the Priestly fountain was much larger and grander perhaps, but it was like an old Victorian lady in a shabby dress. This pond was the essence of classic. Still, secret, nonobtrusive. And better yet, Cody had shoveled out the earth to create it just for her.

The first time she'd seen it had been on the return from their honeymoon, and she'd been equally enchanted with the ambience of the rocks and water and the implied affection of the man who had just married her.

How had she forgotten how much he loved her? How had she doubted his ability to roll with the punches? Had the last few years worn them both down to the point where they forgot how unique and special what they had was?

Love was like the pond. Rocky, tranquil, deep, shallow—frozen over at times, murky at others...

She heard the kitchen door close and knew at any moment Cody would show up. Did he really think she was going to leave him in the middle of the night? That wasn't fair. If she didn't want him jumping to conclusions, then neither should she. She turned to look over her shoulder.

But it was Pauline who approached, dressed in a thick robe belted tight around her waist. She stopped midstep when she saw Cassie.

"Oh, I'm sorry, I didn't mean to bother you," Pauline said. "I didn't know—I'll just go back inside—"

"No, come on, sit down," Cassie said, patting the bench beside her. "It's chilly out here but really peaceful. I just couldn't sleep."

Pauline sat beside Cassie, looking at her at last, full on, eye to eye. "I'm leaving the Open Sky," she said.

Cassie looked deeper into the woman's eyes. "What? You've been here—"

"—since before Cody's mother disappeared, I know."

"Is it because I'm home, because if it is, Pauline, that's not necessary. You and I never had a problem—"

"No, no," Pauline said, patting Cassie's hand. "No, it's not that." She was quiet for a second, and then she added, "Birch told me that Cody talked to him and Adam this morning and told them why you left. I didn't say anything, but I already knew it. Don't be surprised. Your longing for a baby was all over your face. Every time you saw a chick or a duckling or a kitten or a calf or a foal, you just melted. And the way you treated that puppy of yours! Just like she was your baby."

"I didn't know I was that obvious," Cassie said.

"Maybe you weren't—maybe I just saw it. But Cody didn't because Cody didn't want to." She put a hand on Cassie's arm. "He changed after his mother left. He'd been closest to her, and then when she was gone and Birch was so angry, I think it just scared him, so he got real quiet and introspective. Pierce was a little hellion and Adam was the artist, but Cody just devoted himself to the ranch and to taking care of his brothers. And Birch was, well, Birch. Children were meant to follow orders. Pierce coped with his father's stubborn streak by rebelling and ultimately leaving. Adam charmed his way into what he wanted. And Cody just kind of closed up more than ever.

"Then he met you. And I thought, hallelujah, he'll open up again. And he did."

"But parenthood still scared him," Cassie said. "I know. But what does all of this have to do with you leaving?"

Pauline met her gaze and looked away. "I'm going to tell you something I never told anyone before. I'm in love with Birch. Have been since a couple of years after my husband died. I always knew Birch was still in love with his wife, so I never told him. A couple of months ago when we finally figured out what really happened to Melissa, Birch started to thaw a bit and I thought I had—*we* had—a chance for happiness together. But he's still just a stubborn old coot and it's time I get on with things. And that's why I'm so glad you're here for Cody again. You're going to save him from turning into his father."

"That's a tall order for any woman," Cody said from behind them.

Startled, Cassie and Pauline both turned to face him. Cassie didn't know what exactly Pauline saw—probably the young man she'd cared for most of his life, standing there in pajamas and robe. But Cassie saw a tall, handsome, straight figure with starlight on his skin and dark shadows for eyes. He looked like a prince out of a fairy-tale book, perfectly capable of slaying any dragon who wandered across his path.

"How long have you been back there?" Pauline scolded as she stood.

His voice was gentle when he responded. "Long enough." He stepped forward and hugged her. "I'll miss you," he said. "If you really go, that is."

"I'll miss you, too," Pauline said. "Good night to both of you."

Cody looked down at Cassie. "I thought we agreed you wouldn't wander outside by yourself," he said. Bonnie showed up, panting heavily, back from some private dog mission.

"But Emerson Banner is behind bars—"

He offered her a hand. "And what if he wasn't working alone? What if there's someone out there right now with a nightscope—"

She took his hand and awkwardly got to her feet. The

comforting darkness now seemed more like a cloak for a killer. "Okay, you made your point."

THE COURTHOUSE AND THE sheriff's office had shared the same parking lot for decades. Cody knew there were plans for new facilities, but for now too many cars had to pack into too few spaces. In the end they had to park a couple of blocks away and hike back to the office.

The clerk informed them the sheriff had left in a hurry because of a brouhaha at the nearby courthouse, and they would have to wait for his return. They found an out-of-way corner, but Cassie declined to squeeze herself into one of the plastic chairs, choosing to stand instead. Cody staked out a piece of wall next to her.

The lobby was as crowded as the parking lot, filled with people coming and going or just staring vacantly ahead, but one group stood out.

"That's Robert Banner," Cassie said with a nod. "He doesn't look well, though, does he?"

Cody recognized Robert from their brief meeting the day of Vera Priestly's wake, but Cassie was right. The man's face was noticeably thinner, and it added a couple of years to his appearance.

Robert wasn't alone—it appeared the whole Banner clan had come to Woodwind, including an older man with a hawkish nose and a shaved head. To Cody, he had "five-hundred-buck-an-hour lawyer" written all over him.

"Might as well get this over with," Cassie said, and sighing, walked over to the Banners. He trailed along. He didn't trust a single one of them.

She approached Donna. "Any word about Kevin?"

Donna shook her head. "Nothing."

"He's run off with some floozy," Victoria Banner said.

"Mother!"

"I just want you to know I don't have your ring," Cassie added. "I don't know what happened to it. I sent it to your parents, so someone should look for it there."

"Are you accusing us of stealing our own jewelry?" Mrs. Banner huffed.

The lawyer touched her arm and shook his head. "Don't let her engage you, Victoria. The truth will come out in court."

"You and that bastard child of yours are going to rot in jail," Victoria said.

Cody took a step forward. "Now, wait just a damn minute. If you think you—"

But Cassie caught his arm and, when he looked down at her, she shook her head. He allowed her to lead him back to their corner.

"We have to stay calm," she said softly.

"I don't want to stay calm."

"I know. But this isn't the time or place to let her get to us. Man, am I ever going to get away from those people?"

Cody saw Robert disengage himself from his family and approach. "Don't look now," Cody whispered, "but round two is about to start."

Robert was taller than his father and though he possessed much the same aristocratic bearing he was obviously stressed. He offered Cody a quick handshake. "We met briefly at Grandma's wake," he said.

They hadn't exactly met, but Cody let it go and shook the man's hand.

Robert turned his attention to Cassie. Nodding toward his family, he said, "I'm sorry about that."

"It's not your fault."

"She can be harsh."

Cassie didn't respond. "What are you all doing here?" Cody asked.

"That damn Gibbons," Robert growled. "He had us all trot over here as some sort of show of family solidarity. And because we all came from slightly different locations, we had to bring four different cars. What a waste of gas. They won't even let us see him—they say we can wait until this afternoon when he's back in Cherrydell." He drew his hand through his hair as though he'd done it a dozen times already. "I don't have time for this."

Cassie regarded him with concerned eyes. "Are you okay?"

"Just angry. Dad really screwed up. What was he thinking? Never mind, I know what he was thinking. He was thinking poor old Grandma was too addled to know he was robbing her blind."

Cody was a little surprised at the volume and voracity of Robert's speech. Surely he knew his whole family could hear him?

"This hasn't been easy on you, either," Robert added, glancing down at Cassie. "Donna told me what happened out at your house. She said someone shot you."

"The day I got home. Listen, Robert, the deputy yesterday gave us all the impression they were considering additional charges against your father. Do you know anything about that?"

"Gibbons says he thinks the DA is doing his best to build a case against Dad for murder. And he should have reported his gun was missing at the time he found out."

"Your grandmother wasn't shot."

"No, but you were."

Cassie took a step back. Robert seemed to sense her alarm and took a deep breath. Running a hand through his hair again, he sighed. "Frankly, I can't believe Dad had anything to do with trying to harm you. What would he have to gain? There has to be another explanation."

"Did you see him the day before yesterday?" Cody asked.

Robert shook his head. "No, but that's not unusual. I don't live at the house, and I spend most of my time at my restaurant."

"It's a beautiful place," Cassie said. "Your grandmother was so proud of your success. The time she and I went there still sticks out in my memory, every detail of it. She was just beaming at how all your customers loved you."

"Grandma was special," he said, as he plunged his hands in his pockets.

"Yes, she was." Cassie hesitated a second before adding, "I have to ask you something that's been troubling me. Remember the night we searched for something to support what your grandmother thought she witnessed through her window? Your mother was out at the gate. Did she tell you what she was doing out there?"

"I didn't ask her," Robert said.

"But in light of what your grandmother thought she saw, and then what happened to her two days later—"

"Wait a second," Robert said. "We found nothing out there to support Grandma's claims. The police have torn the place apart since her death, and there's never been any indication of a murder out by the fountain or anywhere else. Well, except for Grandma, of course."

"There was a body recovered from the river downstream a few days after her death," Cassie said.

"Who?"

"I don't know. A man apparently too decomposed to identify right away. It was in the paper. I checked the internet this morning and they still haven't identified him. Don't you think that's suspicious?"

He stared at her a second, then kind of laughed. "Yikes, you aren't pulling any punches, are you? You're accusing my mother of murder. And are you suggesting she then turned around and killed her own mother, too?"

"No," Cassie said. "No, that's not what I meant." She sighed heavily and shifted her weight. "It's just that Cody and I have sworn to be honest with each other, and that means we're going to tell the sheriff everything we know. A threat to me is a threat to our baby."

Cody stared at her a second, surprised and unbelievably pleased with her words and the passion with which they were spoken. It felt great to finally be on the same page about *something*. He would have kissed her right then if they'd been alone.

"So, I'm just suggesting you have a genuine dialogue with your mother," she added, "especially in light of your father's predicament, because I'm going to tell the officials everything I know. That's the only way out of this for me, I see that now. Tell her that. It will be better if she's up front and honest, too."

"Well—"

He didn't get any further because at that moment, a new group of people erupted into the waiting room from the outside. This time it was Adam and Echo, the sheriff and the blond teenage boy Cody recognized as Dennis Garvey.

"I didn't do nothin'," Dennis grumbled. With a little nudge from the sheriff, he slumped into a nearby chair.

"Shut up, boy," Inkwell said.

Adam hitched his hands on his waist and stared at the kid and then looked around the room, his gaze skimming past the Banners and doing a double take when he connected with Cody.

Meanwhile, Robert squeezed Cassie's hand. "I'm going to go talk to my mother right now. I'm going to repeat everything you said word for word."

"I don't think you have to," Cody said. "Your whole family has been listening to everything you two said until my family came in here."

"That's your family?" he asked, turning to stare at the newcomers.

"Yes."

After Robert had left, Cody and Cassie moved toward Adam and Echo. "What's going on?" Cody asked.

"The boy made some threats," Adam said.

"What kind of threats?"

"Let's just say he's toying around with avenging the loss of his family's good name."

"Great," Cody said without asking the obvious: *What good name?*

Dennis's hands clenched in his lap. "I was just talking."

The sheriff looked from Adam to Echo. "You folks bringing charges?"

Echo and Adam exchanged meaningful glances as Dennis's gaze fastened on Cassie, in particular her pregnant belly.

"What do you think?" Adam said.

Echo blinked her black eyes and sighed. "I hate to get him in more trouble."

"You sure?" Inkwell barked.

"Yeah, we're sure." Adam looked at Cody and added, "The trial is over. The jury was out all of thirty minutes. Hank Garvey is going away for a while. Dennis was just letting off steam. Right, Dennis?"

Dennis glowered at the world.

"I should charge him for disrupting court," the sheriff said, but Cody could tell his heart wasn't in it. Dennis grew very still as the sheriff added, "Okay, Dennis, instead of jail, you and me are going to have ourselves a nice little chat." Inkwell looked at Cody and added, "You and Cassie mind giving me an hour or so before we talk about your predicament?"

"No problem," Cody said.

"We could go grab an early lunch," Adam suggested. "Echo's car is parked right outside."

"Sounds good to me," Cassie said. "We had to park Cody's big truck down in front of the church."

As the two women discussed restaurant choices, Cody glanced at the Banners.

He wasn't surprised to find Victoria Banner's gaze locked onto Cassie. He wasn't even surprised to see Donna darting pointed looks.

It was the depth of their antagonism that staggered him.

Chapter Ten

Cassie sank into the bucket seat, grateful to be getting out of Woodwind at last. It had been a long afternoon. An hour with the sheriff, who had chastised them for not coming forth with information about the shooting when it first happened, then another two answering questions from Deputy Tucker. There had been times during the interviews where she'd wondered if she was going to wind up in jail after all.

On the plus side, it sounded to her that no one thought she had admitted a killer into Mrs. Priestly's room.

On the minus, there was the fact that she'd been caught with a whole lot of very pricey jewelry that didn't belong to her. That jewelry was part of Mrs. Priestly's estate and as such was being assessed and probated along with everything else.

Plus, it was of interest because of the older woman's murder.

The deputy had informed her that the emerald ring wasn't the only piece still missing. Six diamond necklaces, worth thousands, could not be accounted for.

They wanted her back in Idaho. Her fate was totally up in the air.

Cody's thoughts were obviously running along the same lines as hers. "Why do they keep expecting you to know about this damn jewelry? Isn't it obvious someone at that house is screwing around with it? I can't believe Inkwell told you to go home and search everything you took from the house to try to find the missing pieces. And Deputy Tucker looked like he wanted to slap handcuffs on you when you told him about the explosion at the apartment."

She'd explained how she'd been forced to grab her handbag and run for her life. Both officers had looked at her extended midsection as though trying to picture her fleeing in that manner.

"Fear of death is a great motivator," she'd told them.

The deputy had known about the explosion at the Cherrydell apartment. Thanks to the power of the blast, little evidence had survived the explosion and so it had been racked up to a heater malfunction—not that uncommon an event. Now he said he would inform the fire department, but his square jaw had clenched as though he were trying to figure out if she was telling the truth or lying up a storm. Even if the fire department could determine the explosion had been intentional, how would they know who did it? And Tucker had also pointed out that the landlord had filed an insurance claim, which would mean additional legal issues…

"Deputy Tucker said Emerson Banner is insisting his wife bring charges against me for theft," Cassie said with a shudder. The snowflakes had gotten bigger since they left Woodwind and were beginning to stick.

Cody gunned the engine to climb the upcoming incline and didn't respond until they'd started down the other side. "I guess we'll go through your purse again. It would be great to get this resolved and get these people off your back."

"What did you think when the sheriff admitted the

gun Mr. Banner says was stolen is capable of firing bullets like the ones fired at me?" she asked.

"I guess I wasn't surprised. And the fact he says he spent the day you were shot out hiking by himself looks suspicious. At least now he's behind bars."

"Yes," she said, taking a deep breath. "Maybe the worst of it is over."

"I hope so."

Fallow fields spread out to the right. To the left, heavily forested land came practically to the roadside. They would climb out of this meadow in a few minutes, then travel up a steep hill and make a series of hairpin turns before reaching Open Sky land, which would spread before them with welcoming arms....

"Let's go cut a Christmas tree," Cassie said impulsively.

Cody darted her a glance. "Before Thanksgiving? I thought you hated doing that."

"Not this year. Let's have it all set up for when Pierce and Analise get home. We'll get Adam and Echo to come with us, and maybe Sassy Sally and her veterinarian fiancé."

"Do you really think it's a good idea to go up into the mountains?"

"I'll have you to keep me safe. Besides, Emerson Banner is back in Idaho by now. Time for a little normalcy, don't you think?"

"I was thinking of the baby."

"It'll be okay. We'll take the snowcat and we won't go as far as usual and Echo knows about emergency baby birthing. It was part of her training."

"I don't know why that doesn't comfort me," he said, his voice hesitant. "I guess it's because having a baby in a snowcat seems like a really bad idea."

"I'm not due for almost a month. Please."

"Well, you're right in that a little normalcy would be a welcome respite."

The sound of the tires against the wet pavement was almost hypnotic, and Cassie laid back her head. Normalcy. Would she even know it if she ran into it? It had been a while…

She was close to drifting off when a wobble in the truck shook her back to full consciousness.

She opened her eyes in time to witness a deer jump out of the verge ahead and land on the road in front of the truck. She gasped loudly as Cody yanked the wheel to avoid hitting it. The startled animal disappeared from view as the truck swerved violently into the empty lane beside them. The front dipped, and a terrible grating sound filled their ears. They shot toward the field on the far side of the road.

Air bags deployed the minute the truck hit the ground after jumping the ditch. Cassie was pinned back against her seat, hands clutching the door handle on one side and the back of Cody's seat on the other. She braced herself as well as she could, expecting the truck to continue to fly across the unobstructed land. But it didn't. Instead it plowed ahead, grinding its way along, earth and metal battling each other for supremacy, the contents of the cab flying until at last it all culminated in a heart-jarring stop.

For a second Cassie sat still, waiting for a sign she and Cody—and most of all, their child—had survived yet another violent incident.

And then a hot poker of anger blazed through her shock. This was an accident, what else? But coming on the heels of an explosion and a shooting, it was too much. It was as if fate was wrestling her for her own

future, punishing her, even. She fought against the air
bag until suddenly aware her door had creaked open just
a foot or so. Cody leaned inside as far as he could and
pushed the now-deflated bag out of the way.

"Come on, Cass, let's get clear of here. It's going to
be a tight fit. Can you make it?"

She hadn't realized until the blast of cold air hit her
face that she was crying, sobbing, the tears blurring
everything except her determination to get out of the
truck. With his help and a do-or-die attitude, she was
able to angle herself through the opening at last, and
once again snagged her handbag as she departed. She
erupted into the cold Wyoming dusk, grabbing the side
of the truck to steady her wobbly knees.

Already snow was beginning to accumulate on the
deep furrow the truck had made as it churned its way
across the field. Cody lowered the back gate of the
wildly tilted truck, took off his coat and set it down,
then helped Cassie climb up to sit on top of it where she
perched gratefully, still too shaken to think. He patted
her over quickly, his hands coming to rest on her bulging
stomach as she continued to cry without totally under-
standing why.

"I feel something move," he said at last, and the relief
on his face touched her so deeply it stopped the tears.
She threw herself against his chest and he held her, his
solid warmth a balm, more real to her than the earth and
the stars. He kissed her forehead then her lips, and she
forgot about the snow and just about everything else.

Finally the cold got to her. "Cody? What happened?
Did we hit the deer?"

"I don't think so," he said. "We lost a tire, that I know.
That's why we plowed through the dirt instead of rolling
over it. You're okay?"

"A little shaken."

"And Junior is rolling around in there okay?"

She smiled as her hands rested on the bulge. "Yes."

He nodded once and strode off to circle the truck, pausing near the passenger front end, kneeling down and continuing his perusal as she looked down to brush snow off her tummy. When she glanced back at him, she caught him staring at her, and there was something in his eyes....

Pauline had said Cassie was Cody's salvation but at times, like right this second, it was hard to feel like anything more than a giant burden. She'd spent her youth trying to ease her mother's sadness, and then at the end she'd nursed her through a terminal illness while holding a full-time job managing a feed store office. She'd prided herself on being strong and resilient, and perhaps even more than that, she'd prided herself on being content.

She was not going to live a life of despair, so caught up in disappointments that the years sped by without even being acknowledged as the miracles they were.

And that was why she'd really stayed away when discovering she was pregnant. Coming home to witness Cody's disappointment at the new direction his life had to take would have been too much to bear, too familiar in some gut-wrenching way.

He pulled a phone from his pocket and placed a call as he walked back to her. A minute later, it was obvious he was talking to Adam. He explained where they were and what had happened and asked someone to come fetch Cassie right away. "And get Mike to come out here with a tow rig," he continued.

He listened for a second and shook his head. "Okay,

well, then, can you come? I want to haul the truck back to the ranch tonight."

"Why can't Mike come?" Cassie asked, as he hung up.

"He fell off his horse today and hurt his back. No riding for a week."

"Can't the truck wait until tomorrow?"

"No. Even before the deer, I knew something was wrong."

She blinked away snowflakes. "What do you mean?"

"The steering was loose. There was a shimmy. I was going to pull over and then the deer showed up and we swerved—"

"Cody—what are you saying? This was an accident. The deer…"

He caught her shoulders in his hands. Looking hard into her eyes, he shook his head. "I don't think so, Cass. I think someone tried to kill you—again."

"I'M SORRY, CODY, BUT there's no proof anyone tampered with the tire," Adam said. He was crouched on the barn floor studying the front end of the truck, which he and Cody had towed to the ranch after the crash while Sassy Sally fetched Cassie.

Cody, shadowed by Bonnie, stared down over his brother's shoulder. "What about the lug nuts?"

"What about them?"

"I'm telling you, that tire was tampered with." He straightened up and walked to the workbench where he all but slammed down the wrench. "Someone loosened or removed the lug nuts. They probably left one or two still barely attached so they'd wiggle free as we drove."

"You don't know that," Adam said, as he stood up.

"I know if the deer hadn't caused us to swerve into

the field, we would have lost that tire at the top of Crescent Pass when we took the first hard right, and that would have sent us off a damn cliff."

Adam wiped his hands on a grease rag and stared at the dirt-encrusted axle, which Bonnie was busy sniffing. "I agree the deer was a lucky break," he said, glancing at Cody. "I'm just saying there's no way to prove the lug nuts didn't jiggle loose on their own. This truck hasn't had new tires in a couple of years."

"I know. I thought of that. But I'm not buying it."

"Why don't you call the sheriff? If someone fooled around with your truck, maybe someone else saw it."

"We were parked way down by the old church. Not many people hang around that place on a cold, miserable Thursday afternoon."

"So, you're thinking one of the Banners?"

"Or Dennis Garvey. He was sure staring hard at Cassie."

Adam shrugged. "I don't think he'd try something like this. I really don't think he wants to hurt anyone, let alone a woman with a baby."

"Yeah. I guess it's stretching the imagination to think Cassie could have two killers after her."

"So, who are you thinking? The blond guy?"

"That's Robert. Maybe. He was jumpy today, but his family is falling apart around him. He'd probably know enough about cars to figure out the lug nut thing, and if he's the one after Cassie, then he's been out here before and knows about the roads. You can't overlook his mother, either."

"The tall, classy-looking older woman? She hardly looks like the kind to dirty her hands with sabotage."

"Yeah, except she plays golf all the time. That's a very fit lady. And she hates Cassie with a passion."

"How about the older guy?" Adam asked, leaning against the truck.

"Gibbons, the family lawyer. Seems unlikely he'd get involved in something like this. That leaves the younger woman who is Donna Cooke, Robert's sister. Cassie said Donna works at an auto shop with her husband."

"She looked strong enough to screw around with a lug wrench," Adam said.

"Yeah, she does, and really, she didn't seem all that fond of Cassie, either, despite all her smiles. Plus, Cassie said Donna's husband is missing, so maybe he's in on this in some way." Cody rubbed his eyes and sighed as he settled his backside against the truck and stared down at the cement floor.

"You look like hell," Adam said.

Cody looked up at Adam. "It's been a real long day."

"So, how's it going?"

"How's what going?"

Adam emitted a bark of laughter. "The reconciliation, you dope. You and Cass. Looming parenthood. Your marriage."

Cody rocked his open hand. "So-so."

"She seems as great as always."

"But different, too," Cody said.

"How so?"

Cody shrugged, wishing now he hadn't brought it up. Uncomfortable talking about his feelings, he thought about walking off—but wasn't that what he'd been doing his whole friggin' life?

Adam said, "You know, Cody, I've always looked up to you. I mean, why not? You were the oldest. You had memories of Mom that Pierce and I didn't have. You were there for us when Dad kind of retreated into being bitter. And don't deny it—I know you're the one who twisted Dad's arm and got him to let me change the direction of the ranch, going organic and all natural. To me, in a lot of ways, *you* are the Open Sky."

Cody slid his brother a glance, speechless yet again.

"And I know you paid a price for that," Adam continued. "I know you had too much responsibility, and I always kind of figured that was why a woman like Cassie was so attractive to you. I mean not only is she drop-dead gorgeous, but she's very capable. She needs you, but in a way she doesn't, because she's always been able to take care of herself."

"And now things are way out of her control," Cody mumbled.

"Yeah, they are."

"And if she'd just told me she was pregnant instead of running away I would have coped, and she would never have met these people and none of this would be happening."

"That's a lot of ifs," Adam said after a minute.

"Hell, I know. Cassie came back to me only because she was afraid after the explosion," Cody admitted. "Our deal was she stay until she was safe, until the baby was born. Then we'd renegotiate the future. Lately it seems we've been a little closer."

"So tell me the truth. Are you glad she's back?"

"Yes and no," Cody said with another darted glance. "I love her, you know that."

"But?"

"But I don't know if it's enough."

"And the baby?"

He sighed deeply, staring into the dark corners of the barn. "That's the bottom line, isn't it? The baby. The baby takes away all the options, all the choices. Along with your kids and Pierce's, he or she will be the future of the Open Sky. So, there's really nothing more to say, is there?"

The silence stretched between them for over a minute before Adam clapped him on the shoulder. "You've always been the strong, silent type, big brother. Come on, I'll treat you to a beer. After all this emoting, you must need one."

"Yeah," Cody said, but damned if he didn't feel a little lighter on his feet.

UNCLE PETE HAD WALKED with Cassie out to call the guys in for dinner. He'd become distracted before the barn, though, and had sent her on ahead.

So, she'd been alone when she heard Cody and Adam talking, and she'd paused, caught like a bug in a spider's web—not wanting to hear, unable to move away.

And heard everything.

As their voices stopped, she stepped outside the barn. Pete was tinkering with the snowcat, a fully tracked vehicle with an enclosed cab. She'd mentioned they wanted to use it to go after a Christmas tree. Engrossed in his task, he didn't even look up at her.

By the time Bonnie raced out of the barn and circled her legs, followed closely by Cody and Adam, Cassie had arranged it so it seemed she was just arriving.

"Pauline says dinner is ready," she mumbled, amazed at how ordinary her voice sounded when inside it felt like parts of her were beginning to seize, like neglected machinery in an abandoned factory.

"Did you come out here alone?" Cody asked, his gaze darting into the black yard.

"Uncle Pete is over by the snowcat," she said. Pete looked up and called out that he'd come inside in a few minutes. He was standing under an overhead light that illuminated the falling snow. It appeared to have tapered off.

Cody reached for Cassie's hand. With Adam on his other side and the dog circling them, they walked back to the house.

Although Cassie knew the two men were talking about the herd up at the Hayfork pasture, she didn't hear any details. Her head was filled with the echo of Cody's words: *The baby takes away all the options, all the choices.*

She'd been right to worry about trapping him.

Now what?

Chapter Eleven

Pleading a headache, Cassie went to bed early. She told Cody she was too uncomfortable to sleep with another person—would he mind going back to the other room for the night? He'd agreed, although his expression had revealed confusion.

Nothing she could do about that. Frankly, nothing she wanted to do about it. She needed time to herself, and right now even looking at him made her miserable.

Another week or two and she really wouldn't be able to travel. If she was going to leave, this was it.

She started digging through her closet, looking for things that would fit now and after the baby came. Loose jumpers were about her only choices for now, but she added a couple pairs of jeans and a few sweaters to the stack on the bed for later.

She was buried in the closet going through her shoes when a knock on the door was followed by the creak of it opening and then Cody's voice. "I see your light is on."

She turned quickly into the room with two pairs of boots in her hands.

He looked from the pile of clothing to the shoes to her eyes. "Cass?"

"I need to get rid of some things," she said, wishing

she had the courage to tell him what she'd heard and what she was really thinking. But what was the point? What could he say?

"I thought you had a headache."

"I do have a headache," she snapped. "But people don't just quit doing everything because their head hurts. I'm cleaning out my closet."

He looked taken aback by the strident tone of her voice. "Okay. Well, can I help?" He gestured at the bed. "If you want these things stored or something I'll go get a box and move them for you."

"Those are the things I'm keeping," she said. "And, no, I don't want help."

He took a step back as though her words had actually shoved him. Well hadn't she felt the same way out in that barn?

"Did you search your things again for the jewelry? Do you want an extra pair of eyes?"

"I looked. There's nothing. You know that and I know that. Those people are playing some kind of game and I'm the fall guy."

"I agree. Well, I also wanted you to know everyone is on for the Christmas tree cutting tomorrow. Do you still want to go?"

"Why wouldn't I want to go?" she said, although the truth was she'd forgotten all about it. It was just a Christmas tree, though. So what? What did it matter?

She dropped one of the boots.

How could a tree make any difference?

But it did.

Cody was there in a flash, picking up the boot and handing it to her. "Are you sure you're all right?"

"Do me a favor," she said, as she tucked the boot under her arm. "Leave me alone for a while. I'm just frazzled after what happened tonight. I'll see you in the morning, okay?"

"Okay," he said, his gorgeous dark eyes looking directly into hers. The next thing she knew he'd lowered his head until his lips touched hers and as always, they were molten, they were soft and they made her burn inside.

Unfair tactics! How could he kiss her like that after telling his brother she'd trapped him, she'd taken away his options, she'd ruined his life!

"Good night," he said, and closed the door behind him.

She stood there for a long time, staring at the door while her mind raced though scenarios.

Pack a bag, sneak away into the dark. Leave a note explaining. No, she could not do that to him again.

Go after him. Tell him what she'd overheard. What could he say? She'd misunderstood? No way. The truth? He was making the best of it. What else could she ask of him?

Tell Cody it was too dangerous on this ranch and she needed to go somewhere else to have her baby. He would agree and then he would insist on going with her, which would solve nothing.

Or she could stay here. She could go cut a Christmas tree and make the best of things and have her baby if no one managed to kill her first, and then, when she was stronger and out of danger—leave. Openly and up front. Like an adult. Get a job in Woodwind where Cody would have access to his child. Where her baby could know his or her father. People made these kind of arrangements every single day and she could, too.

Boots spilled from her hands as she sat down on the bed. Would this ever be over?

CODY HELPED CASSIE INTO the passenger seat of the snow-cat. It was a small two-seater, used mainly for moving snow around and transporting people to and from the airstrip during winter months. It wasn't that practical for a ranch but it was something his father had run across a few years earlier, and there was no doubt it came in handy on occasion.

Like this. Echo and Adam were each taking snow-mobiles. He'd drive the snowcat with Cassie, and they could tie the tree to the back of it for the return trip. He had no plans to go far into the mountains—for one thing, the vehicle wasn't great in very steep conditions. They'd go far enough to give the illusion of a journey. He carried a shotgun, and Adam was armed with a rifle in a scabbard. Still, part of him thought the whole idea was risky and frivolous.

But there was no way he was going to disappoint Cassie. She had acted odd the night before and she was acting strange now. Very quiet. Did women get that way right before giving birth? He would watch her like a hawk.

"Where's Sally and her veterinarian?" he asked.

"They're not coming until later, if at all," Cassie said. "Ethan had emergency surgery on a kitten who ate a thread. Wound up around its intestines. He's not sure when or even if he can get here. She's waiting for him at the house."

"Well, since everyone else is at the Garvey sentencing trial, that's probably a good idea," Cody said.

"Why didn't Adam and Echo go to the sentencing?"

"Adam said they don't want to inflame Dennis any-more than he already is. Despite everything, I think they have a soft spot for that kid." He started the engine and they took off, him doing what he could to make the trip as smooth as possible.

But she turned to look out her window and barely spoke. Why?

They came across Adam and Echo a half hour later, parked next to a stand of small to medium Noble fir trees growing on the edge of the forest. He stopped the snowcat and went around to help Cassie out. She immediately sank into the snow. Snowshoes were out for her this year, so she agreed to stay at the cat and point out which tree she wanted. Adam and Cody would cut it down while Bonnie supervised.

"Times such as these," Echo said, as she poured hot chocolate into two mugs, "I rather enjoy being thought of as delicate." She handed Cassie a mug and grinned.

They were seated on the back of the cat. The men were taking turns hacking at the trunk of a fourteen-foot tree a hundred yards away.

Cassie took a sip of the rich, hot liquid. "I'm sick of being delicate," she said.

"I bet you can't wait to get back on a horse. Cody told me you're a wonderful horsewoman."

"I heard you won over Bagels," Cassie said, referring to the feisty gelding everyone had learned to have great respect for. "That's quite an accomplishment."

"We're buds now," Echo said. "Although he did try to more or less kill me the first time I rode him."

"Which is when you first got here and met Adam," Cassie said. "We haven't even talked about your wedding."

"That's because it's going to be a very small affair. Mostly family, a few old friends, you know. Pierce said he and Analise want to get married at the same time we do, so it'll be a double ceremony. We're aiming for after Thanksgiving and before Christmas."

"But Analise is a princess! Doesn't that require a lot of people and at least a little pomp and ceremony?"

"They're going to return to Chatioux in the spring and have a regulation royal wedding then," Echo said. "Right now, what with her father just having passed away, the country is in mourning and it's not appropriate. Next spring, after calving season, we'll all go to Chatioux for the wedding. Won't that be fun?"

Cassie nodded, although there was a stinging sensation behind her nose.

"How about you guys? You have a baby coming. Have you started decorating a nursery?"

"Not really," Cassie said. "But we've discussed using the small bedroom down the hall. Cody has been staying in it lately...."

Echo tilted her head and regarded Cassie closely. "Can I ask you a question?"

"Of course."

"You're kind of different today. Are you feeling all right?"

"Different? How do you mean?"

She shrugged. "Quiet, maybe? Like you've made some kind of decision. I was hoping it was that you're glad to be home and plan on staying. I'm looking forward to getting to know you better."

Cassie had no idea she was so transparent. Did Cody sense a change in her, too? She studied Echo for a few moments, wishing she could bare her soul to this woman who would soon be like a sister—well, not if Cassie left. They wouldn't be like sisters then, because Cassie would be gone. The enormity of what she had to lose struck her like a sledgehammer.

"Cassie?"

"Tell me about Princess Analise."

Echo brushed her short dark hair away from her face. "Okay. Let's see. I met her late in the summer when she and Pierce came home for a while, right after her father died and her brother was coronated. She's very nice. Pierce calls her Snow White, which gives you an indication of what she looks like and how laid back she is. She likes to just be called Analise."

"I figured she had to be pretty down to earth if Pierce fell for her."

"She is. You'll like her." Echo was quiet for a second, then smiled. "Are you avoiding my question, Cassie?"

Cassie took a deep, cold breath. "Has anyone ever tried to kill you, Echo?"

"Not the way someone is going after you," Echo said, her dark eyes serious.

"I think it's getting to me. I'm really beginning to think it's all tied into the dead guy they found in the river."

"Adam told me about that. Have they identified him yet?"

"I checked again this morning. They still don't have a name but they did say he has several tattoos of snakes."

"Snakes? Really? Well, someone should recognize that, right?"

"I was wondering if Donna's husband has snake tattoos. He went missing about the right time. I'm not sure how to ask her."

"No kidding. Maybe you could tell the sheriff and he could ask her."

"Maybe."

Bonnie jumped up beside them, her fur covered with snow. Echo patted her and sighed. "I can't wait to get a dog of our own," she said. "And I really can't wait to be a mother."

Cassie put her arms around Bonnie's neck as the fir tree finally crashed to the snow.

ECHO AND ADAM CONTINUED on up the mountain to look for another tree for their own house. They would drag it behind one of the snowmobiles, Adam announced. Laughing, the two of them took off while Cody helped Cassie into the cat. The trip back to the ranch was still subdued. Cody knew enough to sense something was wrong but he wasn't sure what it was. Stress? Apprehension? The baby?

He started to ask Cassie how she was feeling and stopped himself short. If she wanted to be quiet he would do his best to respect it.

That worked for a few minutes.

"Where do you want to set up the tree?" he asked, which was a dumb question. The tree always went in the living room where the tall windows made an inverted V.

"In the living room by the windows," she said.

"I'll get Mike to help me put the lights on it."

"Mike has a hurt back, remember?"

"He can do it sitting down. He told me was bored; this will keep him occupied. Jamie can haul it into the house. The decorations are in the barn—"

"No they aren't. I packed them in the attic last year."

"That's right."

Silence fell as completely as a curtain at the end of a performance. Minus the applause.

He stopped at the house to let Cassie off, and even though he got the distinct impression she could manage fine without him, he followed her up the stairs in case they were icy. Bonnie darted ahead and round the deck, her nose apparently picking up a scent.

"Cassie, wait," he said, as she reached for the door handle.

She turned to him, eyes as blue as an Alpine lake. "What?"

"Something has happened," he said.

She looked away.

"I thought we weren't going to keep secrets."

"So did I," she said, looking back at him. There was a challenge in her gaze, and he reminded himself that underneath the very pregnant skin of his wife beat the heart of a fierce woman with a mind of her own.

"Cass—" he began.

"Don't," she said, and now her eyes were all but pleading.

"Last night you said you needed time and I gave it to you. But I'm not a fool. I can see that you're preoccupied and upset. If you can't be forthright with me, then who—"

"You're a fine one to talk about speaking your mind," she said, eyes flashing.

Her comment, which made no sense to him, was punctuated by a dog bark. They stared at each other for several seconds, trying to ignore Bonnie, but she was persistent. The bark got closer as the dog rounded the corner of the house, saw them, stopped dead in her tracks and yipped. Then she ran back the way she had come.

There was something urgent in her manner. Cody took off after her, aware Cassie followed behind. Now what?

The pond he'd built Cassie was up ahead. It looked as quiet and dormant as it had the day before and the day before that. He saw nothing that would explain the dog's behavior.

Bonnie stood at the far end of the pond where the rocks overhung the bank and the bright yellow leaves of a small aspen tree hovered low over the water. The dog barked again. As Cody moved closer to her, Bonnie leaped into the pond and paddled toward the deepest of shadows.

"Bonnie, get out of there," Cody called.

"Ssh," Cassie said, holding a finger to her lips. "Do you hear that?"

He listened for a second, but all he heard was the splash of the water as the dog paddled around like a beaver.

And then he heard a stifled cry.

Cassie moved closer to him. "What is that? An animal or what?"

"I don't know." Pulling off his boots and shrugging off his jacket, Cody lowered himself into the water, pushing the dog out of the way, vaguely aware that she swam past him to the edge and hauled herself out. The water was chest high and very cold. He moved aside branches until a shocked white face appeared in the dim light, staring through the branches, eyes wide with terror.

"Sally!" he said, moving quickly now to get to her. The right side of her face was covered with blood, her fair hair matted. How long had she been in the water? He asked her this as he worked to loosen her hands from her stranglehold on the tree and rocks, but she could do little more than shake. At least the way she'd wedged herself into the branches kept her shoulders and head out of the water.

"Call Jamie for help," Cody yelled over his shoulder. "His cell number is by the phone in the kitchen."

As he yelled this, he finally managed to pry Sally's hands free and unhook her elbow, then floated her gently toward the side, being careful to keep her head as dry as possible. He knew what to do in these cases—one did not grow up surrounded by cold water without learning the basics. He could hardly believe it when he heard pounding steps and looked up to find Jamie already approaching, moving pretty damn fast for a guy over sixty with bowed legs.

"I was in the office looking for that blasted invoice for the pump— Lord Almighty, is that Sally?"

"Help me lift her out," Cody called. "Keep her horizontal," he added. "Hear me, Sally? Don't try to stand." He was unsure if she understood him, but he'd read that jerking the heart back into full action too quickly could overstress a muscle suffering from hypothermia.

Cassie showed up, carrying blankets, and stood by as Cody and Jamie lifted Sally out of the water, keeping her flat. Together, the two men carried her inside the house, the ends of her long hair and her clothes dripping as they moved through the kitchen to the dining room and beyond into the living area.

Jamie and Cody gently laid Sally on the leather sofa. Cassie was right behind them, and she immediately covered Sally with blankets, tucking them close around her quaking shoulders and wrapping one around her head.

"I'll build up the fire," Jamie said, as Cody grabbed an extra blanket and ran into the kitchen. He found Bonnie camped out on her pillow and hurriedly floated the blanket over her wet fur.

Warm tap water went into one of the red mugs kept on the counter. By the time he got back to the living room,

Jamie had called for an ambulance and was now trying to reach Sally's fiancé. Cassie had all but buried Sally under a mountain of warm blankets and held a towel on her face. Bright red blood seeped through the cotton.

"We need ice," Cassie said softly, glancing up at him. "There are at least two wounds on her scalp and it looks as if her ear was nicked. I think we should keep them cold."

He gave Cassie the mug and went back for an ice bag, wishing Echo or Pauline were around. Both of them knew a lot more about where things were kept than he did. The dog watched him with grave brown eyes from beneath the tent of her blanket as he opened every cupboard and drawer. Eventually he found the ice bag, filled it and returned to the living room.

As Cassie held the bag on Sally's facial wounds, Cody sat down on the edge of the big table.

"What happened?" Sally asked through chattering teeth. "Ethan?"

"Was he here?" Cassie asked, and Cody heard the fear in her voice. Did she flash on a sudden image of Sally's fiancé laying on the bottom of the pond with a smashed skull? That couldn't be. Cody would have run into his body when he moved through the water.

Sally tried to shake her head and winced. "No. He… he didn't come." Tears spilled from her eyes.

"Can you remember anything else?" Cody asked.

She closed her eyes as if trying to think. Finally, lashes fluttering against her cheeks, she whispered, "I went to sit…by the pond…to…to wait for him."

"And you fell in—"

"No." Her blue eyes opened wide and she looked up at Cassie. "Burning on my head. I…I started to turn. Another hit. The water…so cold. Footsteps…"

"You heard footsteps so you hid under the aspen branches?" Cassie said, her voice a whisper.

Sally nodded.

"What happened next?"

"Shoes."

"Shoes?" Cody repeated.

"You saw shoes?" Cassie asked.

Sally nodded. "White…running…"

"White running shoes."

Another nod. "And a…a…gun. White…grrr…"

"Grip?" Cody asked, exchanging a quick look with Cassie. "It had a white grip?"

Sally nodded again.

Emerson Banner's gun!

"Was it a man or a woman?" Cassie asked.

She shook her head gently. "I don't…"

"That's okay," Cassie said soothingly.

"I heard…an…engine."

"That might have been me coming back from the parts store," Jamie said. "That damn pump is out again."

"When did you get back?" Cody asked.

"Twenty minutes ago, maybe?"

"Right before we returned," Cody said. That meant Sally probably hadn't been in the water that long. "Did you see anyone else around?" he asked Jamie.

"No one. 'Course, I wasn't looking, and if a fella ran around the deck and left from the back, I wouldn't of seen 'em."

"Someone shot her," Cassie said, her voice soft. "Sally, do you have any idea who would want to hurt you?"

"No," Sally whispered, as though the gunman might be close by. Her hands suddenly struggled under the blankets and she clutched at her throat. A second later

Cody helped her pull loose a sodden length of blue silk from under the covers.

"That's my old scarf," Cassie whispered.

Cassie's blue scarf...

Cody's gaze met Sally's and then Cassie's, and he saw in both women's eyes the same conclusion that he'd reached himself.

Sally wasn't the gunman's intended victim.

Cassie was.

Chapter Twelve

Sheriff Inkwell looked worn out. He was always a little on the scruffy side, but the long afternoon had taken a toll on him. Even his unruly hair seemed to have wilted over his forehead.

Cassie told him about the dead man in the Idaho river, and he'd assured her it wasn't Kevin Cooke. Donna had reported her husband had one tattoo, and that was on his left wrist. It was a heart with her initials in it.

And she'd also told him Sally's description of the gun. Ivory grips.

"Sounds like Banner's stolen piece," he'd agreed, and then he'd gone with Cody to drain the pond.

Cassie found someone had retrieved the boxes of ornaments and stacked them near the tree on which Jamie, bless his heart, had strung a thousand little white lights. She'd opened a box and settled her frazzled nerves by hanging the glass balls and spiral icicles on the branches.

The EMTs had also checked out Cassie before taking off, and that had been at Cody's insistence. She was fine, the baby was fine, everything and everyone was fine, except no one was fine.

After she answered a few of the sheriff's questions, she stared into her distorted face, courtesy of the reflection in a silver ball, and got lost in thought.

Someone had tried to kill her again, only this time they hurt Sally. Blond hair, blue scarf—she supposed it was possible from the back the shooter could have mixed them up. Not from a front view or the side, however, so whoever had done this had come across Sally after she sat down on the bench.

Cody said it was an example of the same ineptness that had plagued her would-be assassin from the start. But sooner or later, the odds were this person would get it right.

The sheriff had announced they'd found two bullets in the pond, which had now been drained. The casings matched those Cody had discovered up on the hill after the first attempt. Same gunman. Or woman. Same poor choice in a weapon. Ballistic tests would be run if they ever recovered Emerson Banner's gun, but the fact was he had a damn good alibi this time—he was in jail.

Someone touched her shoulder and she shivered. Echo stood behind her holding a mug with a spoon propped up in it. "The tree looks wonderful. I can't wait to put ours up. Adam wants to decorate it with things from the forest, you know, like pine cones and thorns." She handed Cassie the mug. "Pauline made you chicken soup. She said it's Pierce's favorite."

"The kind with little dumplings?" Cassie asked, as she took the mug and settled herself in a chair by the fire. "It smells heavenly."

Echo perched on her heels to hang ornaments on the lower branches Cassie couldn't bend to reach. As Cassie ate her soup she was overwhelmed with how comfortable it all seemed.

The phone rang, and Echo popped to her feet to get it. Cassie tried not to be envious. She couldn't remember the last time she'd popped out of a chair.

Echo spoke briefly into the receiver and then brought it to Cassie, mouthing *It's Donna* as she handed it over.

Cassie was really glad she knew the dead man wasn't Donna's husband. But she couldn't imagine what Donna wanted. "Hello?"

"Where's my ring?" Donna demanded.

"Not that again," she groaned.

"That ring means a lot to me. It's worth a ton of money."

"Like I told you, I addressed the envelope to your parents. Ask them where it is."

"Mother said Father opened the package."

"Your father was embezzling money from your grandmother, Donna. He isn't the most honest person on the planet."

There was a long pause before Cassie heard a gruff "Maybe not, but maybe you aren't, either!" Then Donna hung up abruptly.

Echo looked up from her task, a ten-inch crystal snowflake dangling from her fingers. "What did she want?"

"She's still positive I stole that ring from her. That whole family is crazy."

The phone rang again as Cassie set it down. She answered it with another hello. Caller ID had informed her the area code was Idaho, though the rest of the number was unknown to her. She just hoped it wasn't Donna calling back to throw more accusations.

"Is Cassie there?" a male voice asked.

"Is that you, Robert?"

He paused for a second. "Cassie. I didn't recognize your voice. Is everything okay?"

"It's been a long evening," she admitted. "Someone shot at a friend of ours. What can I do for you?"

"I talked to my mother about why she was outside that night. Remember, you asked me to? Her excuse is a little far-fetched."

"What did she say?"

"She said she'd read in the paper that some comet was going to be visible in the middle of the night and she could see it better down where the branches in the garden didn't obscure the sky."

"A comet?"

"I know." He laughed without mirth. "I didn't believe it, either, but here's the thing. I checked and there was one."

"But it was overcast and raining, remember?"

"Mother insisted it was clear for a few minutes, and that's why she went down there."

Was that possible? Cassie had been asleep before Mrs. Priestly's summons for help. Maybe the sky had cleared for a while. "Do you believe her?"

"To tell you the truth, right about now I don't know who to believe." He paused for a second before adding, "I have a huge favor to ask."

She didn't like the sound of that and was pretty sure where he was headed. "I've searched everywhere for the jewels," she said, hoping to preempt his request. "I simply don't have them. Not the emerald or any diamonds—"

"No, no, not that, I told you, they seem like small potatoes to me right now."

"Well, they're not small potatoes to your parents or your sister. I'd just as soon not give birth in a jail cell."

He laughed again. This time it was brittle. "That's not going to happen," he insisted. "But my favor is pretty big considering everything, and I can't think of a single reason you should agree to it except I really need you to help me. I need to talk to you. Things are so dismal around here I can't get away…I know you're very pregnant, but will you come to my restaurant tomorrow? I'll treat you to a nice lunch."

She hesitated long enough that he continued. "I know you're not my sister, but I can talk to you and I can't talk to Donna, not about this."

"Why? Is it about her?"

This time he hesitated, and then it sounded to Cassie as though he closed a door. His voice dropped a notch. "Yes, it's about Donna. You know her husband is still missing, right?"

"I assumed."

"I'm not sure he *is* missing."

"She just called here, right before you," Cassie said. "If you know she's done something, tell the police."

"No, no, I may be wrong. I need a clear head. Too much is happening. Please, Cassie. I know you're not family, but it's hard to overlook the way your life is mixed up with ours. Will you come?"

She started to say no, but just then Cody crossed the room on his way to the den, Bonnie trotting along behind him. The anxious look he darted her way irritated the heck out of her. Before overhearing his conversation with Adam, she'd assumed his anxiety was for her safety and that of their baby. Now she wondered if it was more about himself. *He was stuck…*

She whispered "Okay" into the phone.

"That's great. Around noon?"

"Isn't that a busy time for you?"

"Not lately. See you tomorrow."

She clicked off the phone and got to her feet to resume trimming the tree with Echo. As she took care of the branches she could easily reach, she made a mental list of the reasons she would likely cancel the visit when sanity reasserted itself in the morning.

Number one: Could she drive that far? Did it make any sense at all to chance such a thing?

Number two: Could she trust Robert?

Number three: Someone was trying to kill her. No reason to make it easier on that someone by parading around by herself, and in Cherrydell of all places.

The sheriff ducked back into the room. "I'm heading out," he said. "I'd appreciate it if you stayed inside the house tonight, Mrs. Westin. Considering the looks of that wheel on your truck, I'm having a hard time believing the bullet today wasn't meant for you."

"I'll stay inside," she assured him.

Echo walked back into the kitchen with the sheriff as Cody came out of the office. He looked at Cassie a long moment, hands jammed in his pockets. "The tree looks great. I'll get a ladder and finish the top if you like."

"Sure."

"Who was on the phone?"

Now he was checking up on her?

"Let me rephrase that," he said. "Was it the hospital about Sally?"

"Uh, no."

"I'll go get the ladder."

"Did Cassie seem odd to you today?" Cody asked Adam a few minutes later. He'd found his brother refilling the pond from a hose, since the sheriff's department was finished with it. Not long from now, the pond, like the lake, would freeze over for the winter. The uninsulated outbuilding pipes would freeze, too, for that matter, and filling the pond would be next to impossible until spring.

"She might have been a little quiet," Adam said.

"She's been that way since after the wreck last night."

"Maybe it rattled her more than she let on."

Cody stared at the stream of water for a few minutes. "She seems mad to me. Mad *at* me. Maybe she blames me for not keeping her safe. It was my big sales pitch, right? *Come back with me, I'll keep you safe.* Hell of a job I'm doing." He rubbed the back of his neck.

"When did she start acting mad?"

"Last night. After dinner. Maybe even before dinner."

"Like when she came to the barn to get us?"

Cody thought back and nodded, then he groaned. "You don't think—"

"That she overheard you telling me you didn't have any choices about being a father? What do you think?"

Now Cody swore softly. "I think I blew it."

Adam chuckled, which irritated the heck out of Cody. "What's so funny?"

"You. You spend your whole life keeping your feelings all bottled up, and then you get down-home honest one time and it bites you in the ass. Big brother, that just sucks."

"Well, I'm glad you're getting a laugh out of it," Cody said, as he grabbed the hose from Adam.

Adam grabbed the hose back. "So use your head."

"Will you just stop talking in riddles?" Cody snapped. "Will you do that for me?"

"Go inside and talk to her. Explain."

"How do I explain—"

"Just do it. Now, or I'll turn this hose on you."

Cody jammed his hands into his pocket where his fingers grazed the jewelry box he'd taken from the safe a few minutes before. He'd planned on giving Cassie the ring, but then it had seemed to him she might view it as a bribe. He went back inside the house. Cassie was still decorating the tree.

"Will you please come with me for a minute?" he asked.

"Where's the ladder?"

"I'll get it later. Please, come with me."

She set aside a garland of silver leaves and followed him into the office. He closed the door behind them, locking it as well.

"Sit down," he said, and she took one of the leather wingbacks. He perched on the edge of the other, forearms resting on his knees as he looked at her.

"Did you hear me talking to Adam last night?" he blurted out, wishing he'd found a graceful way to segue into the topic but knowing he lacked the patience to accomplish such a thing.

She folded her hands on top of their baby and met his gaze. "Yes."

"Did you hear everything?" he asked.

"I heard enough to figure out that you have resigned yourself to starting a family. I wouldn't expect any less of you, but you have to understand, the thought of being married to a martyr doesn't do a lot for me."

"Listen, taken out of context—"

"Oh, no, don't try that. I heard the context. You blame me for everything that's happening. I've ruined your peaceful, self-indulgent, solitary existence that used to come complete with a no-fuss wife. You don't trust me and what's worse, you don't trust yourself, and what's even worse than all that is that I'm too damn pregnant and frightened to walk away. Again."

"If you heard all that, then you heard me say that I love you. That hasn't changed. That will never change."

"I also heard you say you weren't sure love was enough."

He *had* said that. He could remember the words leaving his lips, and he could remember wondering if he was talking gibberish because if love wasn't enough in this world, what was?

And it was like she read his mind. "Love doesn't mean much if it's not supported by trust and commitment. That's what I took your comment to mean."

He saw the hurt in her eyes, heard it in her voice. He'd caused it. In a heart-pounding flash of intense fear, he was on the floor, on his knees in front of her, arms wrapped around her middle, head on her stomach and damn if his eyes didn't sting.

"Cass, stop, please," he said, not sure his mumbling was even audible. "Okay, I said those things to Adam because they'd been chasing themselves around in my head and I didn't want to say them to you. It was like I had to get them out to get past them. But, Cassie, I love you. You're my wife. I'll do anything to keep you safe, to make you happy."

Her fingers touched the top of his head, then her hand slid down his face. He straightened up, and for several seconds they were eye to eye, her hand on his cheek, one of his arms still wrapped around as much of her as he could reach. He saw the fluttering of her heartbeat in her throat, the blush of her lips, the moistness of tears on her lashes.

"I don't want to live without you," he said, and the truth of the words hit him like a fire wall.

"I don't want to live without you, either," she gulped.

He cupped her cheeks, ran his fingers back through her hair, loosening the pins so the spun gold could fall around her face. The muscles in his arms and shoulders quaked with a surge of emotions that shook his core like the heart of an erupting volcano.

"Since the minute I laid eyes on you, you've been the center of my universe," he said, startled with himself for expressing it like that. "When you left, the world was dreary. I didn't know how I was going to get through another day. I think part of me can't believe you could ever love me like I love you."

"I know," she said. "That's the heritage you carry around. That you and your brothers always carried."

"But we know the truth now—"

"Maybe intellectually, but there's part of you deep down that doesn't trust it. That's the irony of all this."

He leaned into her until their mouths connected. When her tongue touched his lips, it fanned that internal inferno.

He wanted to claim her, mate with her in a way that seemed almost primal. Not for ownership of her body, but of her heart—nothing less than total submission on both their parts was ever, ever going to be enough for him.

He ran a hand across her breasts, slid fingers between the buttons of her dress, connected with her warm flesh. She was fuller than before, softer. What he wouldn't give to nestle his face in her cleavage. In fact, the nestling of body parts was suddenly all he could think about.

There was a wariness in her body still, a watchfulness. He wanted to drive it away.

He kissed her again and again, levering himself over her as she leaned back in the chair, every part of his anatomy swelling and throbbing with painful, exquisite desire, his need for her as acute as a drowning man's need for a gulp of air.

And something about that need apparently got through

to her, because her hands slid up under his shirt and across his back, across his hot skin and toward his waist.

How could being with her seem so familiar and so alien at the same time? Where did the dream stop and reality begin?

"You are incredibly sexy," he rasped against her ear.

"Belly and all?" she whispered back.

"Belly and all. I want you, Cass."

"I don't know…"

"Tell me to stop and I will."

She didn't say a word.

That was all he needed. Within seconds, he'd unbuttoned her dress from neck to hem, and as his hands touched every beautiful, exposed inch of her skin, she fumbled with his belt and zipper. When her hands touched his engorged flesh, he all but came right then, but he reined himself in, freeing her of her underwear, delighting in the changes her body had undergone, the ripening, the richness, that softened her angles.

"Oh, Cody, I've been afraid—"

"No more fear," he whispered as his anxious hands roamed her curves. His lips and tongue explored every detail of her until her soft, satiated cries washed through his gut.

And as he wondered how he was going to find the same release, she scooted to the edge of the chair and pulled him against her. All the treasures that were hers to give were there for the taking, and he was dizzy with lust. He came to her carefully, crazy with desire.

"It's okay," she gasped against his neck. "You're not hurting me."

And for the first time in months, he let him himself go…

SHE AWOKE EARLY, even before the light hit the window. Her first thought was of Cody, and she turned her head to look at him. He was barely visible in the glow from the nearby night-light.

Sex had been a mistake. Being swept up in his need had superseded her better sense. Sex never really fixed anything; she knew that, but she was pretty sure Cody didn't. He probably thought everything was all better, all their problems were behind them. Wasn't that how men tended to think?

He'd hate her when he realized that the words he'd spoken to Adam still rang louder in her ears than his explanations.

How could she go to Cherrydell and meet with Robert? How could she leave the ranch without telling Cody? But how could she tell him and risk him saying no, which would make her furious and ruin everything they were struggling so hard to rebuild?

Bottom line: Was it dangerous? She did not intend to be stupid, but curiosity about what Robert needed to discuss concerning his sister was eating away at her. If he knew something that would help stop this madness, didn't she have to go find out what it was?

Didn't she owe that to Cody and their baby—and to Sassy Sally, for that matter?

She got out of bed carefully, trying her best not to rouse Cody. He looked beautiful in the dim light, his dark head on the pillow, his features soft in repose. And even though she accepted the paradox of it all, she felt a little faint with her desire for him.

Hormones. Damn their greedy hearts…

Dressing carefully, she went downstairs, delighting in the sight of the decorated Christmas tree. The laptop was sitting on the counter in the kitchen, and she brought it to the island after starting a pot of decaf coffee.

A call to the hospital revealed they were holding Sally for a day or two because of the head injuries, but she was expected to make a full recovery. That was a huge relief to Cassie.

Settling herself on a stool, Cassie typed "Idaho drowning victim, identity unknown," into the search engine and up popped her man…so to say.

It was a news article dated just that morning. The body had been identified as a drug dealer named Bennie Yates. The rest of the article was a rehash of the snake tattoos, five on the torso, three on the arms, one descending to the back of his hand.

The back of his hand.

Why did that give her pause?

She heard a noise at the door and looked up, momentarily spooked, but the door quickly opened and Pauline came inside, wearing just slippers and a robe.

What had gone wrong now?

Chapter Thirteen

"I didn't expect anyone to be up," Pauline said.

"I couldn't sleep," Cassie explained.

"Any word on Sally?"

"They say she'll be fine. Is something wrong?"

"Wrong? Oh, you mean because I was outside in my robe. No, everything is fine, or at least what passes for fine around here lately." She immediately turned her attention to grabbing cups from the mug rack and setting two on the island. She poured coffee, slid one carefully to Cassie, picked hers up, looked back at Cassie and set it down so abruptly the contents sloshed over the lip.

"I can't lie," she said. "I was *with* Birch."

"You mean—"

Pauline nodded as she mopped the spilt coffee with a dishrag.

"For the first time?"

"Heavens no, although he usually comes to my room. I went out there last night to tell him I was leaving the Open Sky and he asked me to stay and I said I couldn't, and then the most amazing thing happened."

Cassie smiled as she lifted the mug to her lips. "What?"

"He asked me to marry him. He said the preacher was

going to be here to marry Adam and Echo and Pierce and the princess so why not me and him, too?"

"I knew it!" Cassie said, as she set the mug down. "Oh, Pauline! What did you say?"

"I said I'd think about it," the older woman announced, and winking, picked up her cup and sashayed out of the kitchen toward her room.

Cassie closed the laptop and propped her chin on the heel of her hand. If they could just put an end to all the violence and find the missing jewels, then things around the Open Sky would look pretty darn rosy. There would be new marriages everywhere you looked, and that would mean renewed energy and enthusiasm and, eventually, from the two younger couples, children for her son or daughter to play with. And more than anything, there would be Cody, strong and sexy...

She wanted that future with a vengeance, and yet there were obstacles. An external one in the form of a would-be murderer and thief; an internal one in the form of trust...

She would not give up on overcoming either of those impediments.

She would go to Cherrydell.

But she wouldn't go alone.

CODY WASN'T THRILLED to be traveling to Cherrydell. Not only were there a million details to iron out before riding out to get the herd, but the thought of Cassie back in Idaho filled him with dread.

And he didn't trust Robert. How did they know this wasn't some elaborate plan to get her back here so the Idaho police could arrest her for theft or worse?

And what if he was the bad guy? Was he delivering her into the lion's den?

But she had asked him to take her. She'd *asked* him. And that meant the world to him. No way would he disappoint her.

"Where is this restaurant?" he asked, as a sign announced Cherrydell, Next Two Exits.

"Take the second turnoff. It's out on the river."

"Is the food any good?"

"I ate there just once. I had butternut soup and it was delicious."

"Ah, soup."

"Don't worry," she said with what he took to be a fond smile. "They have other things like cheeseburgers, okay?"

He knew it was too easy to say that a night of unbridled passion could mend every rift, but for him it had gone a long way toward cementing what they had, what they'd always had, and that was a very strong physical connection. And that physical connection overflowed into every other aspect of their lives. It was what made them, them.

But she was still reserved in that way she had, as though waiting to see what else he had to offer.

"Turn left up there," she added. "It's the wood building on the right."

"Nice place," he said. Built on a bluff near a bend in the river, the restaurant was a single-story wood structure with large windows. A sign over the door announced: River's Nest. Cody parked among a few other cars.

"Not many customers," he said.

"No, there aren't. Last time I was here the place was bustling. Robert said it hasn't been busy lately. I wonder what's going on?" She stared at the empty lot for a second. "I think I should go alone."

"Now, wait a second—"

"Cody, listen. Robert doesn't know you well. He's asked me to come as a friend. Obviously, things are going poorly for him. What's the point of being here if he won't open up to me because he's nervous about talking in front of you?"

"I see your point," he said reluctantly. "How about I wait in the bar?"

"That would be great."

There was no one behind the desk inside the door. Two couples sat at widely spaced tables in the dining room. Through the windows, they could see a deck where additional seating was undoubtedly available during warmer weather, and, beyond that and far below, the silver glint that marked the river.

They walked into the heavily paneled bar, where they found a man behind the counter and another two nursing beers in front of it. "Can I help you folks?" the bartender asked, as they paused in the doorway.

"I have an appointment with Mr. Banner," Cassie told him.

He looked from her bulging middle to Cody and nodded. "Go on down the hall. His office—"

"I know where it is," she said. "Thanks." She squeezed Cody's hand and moved off toward a hallway at the far end of the bar. Cody took a stool and ordered black coffee.

THE LONG, DARK HALL behind the bar jogged a few times before concluding at an outside exit that was kept locked from the inside. Cassie knew this because on the day she'd come to find Robert to tell him his grandmother was waiting in the dining room she'd gotten lost back here and had tried every door. Today she went directly to Robert's office.

When there was no response to her light tap, she tried the knob, which turned easily in her hand. She called out his name as she inched the door open.

The office was small enough to tell her it was empty in a glance. She did notice a narrow opening to the left, but she wasn't sure what to do. Maybe the opening led to a washroom or something. She looked a little closer and caught a glimpse of natural light coming from the end of a short passage and a whiff of fresh air beyond. It must be another exit.

She called Robert's name again. When there was still no answer, she became concerned and, taking a steadying breath, stepped into the new hallway, an ominous feeling pulling her forward.

The outside door emptied onto an attached, small private deck about ten feet square. A backless bench bolted to the deck stood near the edge, located where the deck jutted farthest out over the gorge. Robert Banner lay atop this bench, dressed in a dark suit, blond hair whipping around his face, eyes closed, hands crossed on his chest.

For one interminable moment, he looked like a sacrifice.

And then he turned his head as if sensing her presence and looked right at her.

"Cassie! Is it noon already?" He sat up. It was windy on the gorge and very cold, but he seemed oblivious to the elements. He reached out a hand and she approached cautiously. That bench really was close to the railing, which seemed too frail considering the drop beyond.

He took her hand when she was close enough and pulled her to sit beside him.

"It's a little breezy out here," she said, glad she'd braided her hair that morning. Still, long tendrils were already working loose and blowing everywhere.

"I hope you don't mind," he said. "This little patio is my sanctuary. Did you see the restaurant?"

"It's not as busy as it was the last time I was here."

"My chef quit. He said he didn't want to be associated with the Banner name—it might ruin his reputation. The whole town feels that way."

"You'll survive this," she said. "It'll work out."

He hadn't released her hand yet, and now he squeezed even harder. "I hope you're right," he said, his voice shaky.

"Robert, are you sleeping okay?" she asked, as she took in the dark circles that sagged beneath his eyes. He looked more wasted than he had two days before.

A hasty "Yeah" was followed by a choked laugh. "Who am I trying to kid? No. I'm not sleeping worth a damn."

"Maybe you need to talk to someone," she said, as tactfully as she could. She withdrew her hand and held onto the bench.

"What's the point? Everything is falling apart."

"I know it must seem that way now," she said. "But this is *your* place, not your family's, and things will improve."

"For all intents and purposes my parents own this restaurant," he said.

"I had no idea."

"Well, you're the only one around here who doesn't." He rose abruptly, standing between the fence and rail. His expression went from pained to angry. "I won't drag you through all the finances. Suffice it to say that people don't want to support a family under suspicion of murdering their own matriarch."

"Do you think your father killed your grandmother?"

"No," Robert said. "Why would he? Grandma's death made everything worse for him. All his underhanded dealings came out right into the open. Why focus that attention on himself when keeping her alive meant he'd have time to either figure out how to replace the money he took or talk her into a face-saving compromise of some kind?"

He'd said he wanted to talk about Donna. That was why she'd come, and suddenly she wished she hadn't made Cody linger in the bar. "I can't stay long. Tell me about Donna."

"She found out her husband ran off with another woman," he said, "just like Mom told her he did. She's livid. Who knows what she'll do? But her first goal is getting money, and I think she has her sights set on you and your husband. She's staying with my mother and they plot and plan. I think Donna is framing you so she can then try to buy you off."

"You mean like blackmailing me?"

"Something like that. She was out here yesterday and she was acting crazy." He shook his head as though trying to banish bad thoughts. Then his voice grew soft, he looked out over the gorge and added, "Sometimes I just want to take a flying leap off this deck."

"Robert! Don't talk like that." She stood beside him, grabbing the railing for support but released it at once when it wobbled. She took Robert's arm and tugged. "Come away from here."

He didn't seem to hear her. "I mean it. A few weeks ago I had a good business and a decent family. Now my grandmother is dead, my father is in jail, my mother is pressuring me to repay my loan so she can afford Dad's defense. She even fired the maid. Can you imagine her washing her own dishes?"

"What do you mean she can't afford your father's defense? Isn't she set to inherit a boatload of money? Aren't all of you?"

"Grandma's murder is under police investigation, plus my mother is the executor of her estate and she's a suspect. The lawyers are going to have a field day with this. And right now, no money is going anywhere. Everything is up in the air." He pounded on the railing and made a desperate sound somewhere between a cry and a shout.

"Robert, come away from that railing," Cassie said, stepping close with the intention of grabbing his sleeve.

He clutched the railing even tighter and shook it as though trying to punish it for all the anxiety he felt inside himself.

"Robert—"

A loud cracking noise heralded a section of the railing breaking off into Robert's hands.

Cassie screamed as she reached for him.

His momentum had been such that he swung forward. One leg hung over the near vertical drop as he grabbed for something to stop him from falling. Cassie had been holding his arm, and she slipped forward with him now. One of his hands grasped her wrist. The other clutched a piece of railing that was still intact—for the moment.

Cassie knew she wasn't strong enough to stop his fall if the railing gave way. She would fall, too. She was headed for the edge. The cold air seemed to reach up and pull—

"Hold on!" a new voice yelled, and she managed to

look from under her arm to see a pair of boots she would have known anywhere.

"Cody," she gasped. The fact he was there gave her the strength she needed as he reached around her and grabbed Robert's hand, taking the floundering man's weight himself. Cassie sagged with relief as Cody hauled Robert quickly and efficiently to safety. Robert collapsed onto the bench.

Cassie's hair had come free and now flew around her face. Cody held her for a long moment. "I have to admit I was standing right outside his office when I heard you scream," he said. "I came as fast as I could." He gripped her shoulders and walked her away from the edge. She more or less planted herself against the security of the restaurant as Cody turned to Robert.

"What in the world were you doing?" Cody yelled. "Are you nuts?"

Robert stood with his back to them as he gazed through the gaping hole. "Cody, go hold on to him," Cassie said softly.

Cody walked quickly toward Robert and snagged him by the arm.

Robert looked from the yawning break to Cody and then back to Cassie. "Are you okay?" he asked, as he lurched around the bench toward her. "I'm so sorry. I don't know how that could have happened. Thank goodness your husband was here."

"It's not your fault," she said, hugging herself.

Cody had remained near the damaged area and now squatted, resting his butt on his heels as he examined the wood. When he stood, his expression was fierce. "Who knows you come out here?" he asked, his gaze burrowing in on Robert.

"Everyone. Why?"

"Because I think this railing has been tampered with," Cody said, moving back to Cassie's side. "Anyone want you dead, Mr. Banner?"

Chapter Fourteen

"I just want to take you home," Cody said an hour later. He'd made himself sit through lunch because he'd felt sorry for Robert. But Robert had pushed his food around on the plate as he apologized over and over again.

The man looked like he needed a stiff drink or a week in the hospital—maybe both.

And now Cassie was insisting they drive to the Priestly house.

"With any luck, I'll never come back here again," she said from her seat beside him. "But Robert is in some kind of serious trouble and he needs help, and I can't think of anyone to do that except his mother."

"She doesn't seem like the real motherly type," Cody said. They were driving through the old-town area of Cherrydell, only this time it was midafternoon and all the shops were open.

"She's all he has. Robert needs help before he takes a leap off that deck. Besides, I want to see Donna, and apparently she's staying with her mother."

She then proceeded to tell him Robert's theory about Donna plotting to try to get a payoff from them.

"That makes little or no sense," Cody said. "The jewelry is part of an estate, and it will have to be accounted for. It's not Donna's to fool around with. She can't legally excuse you from its theft."

"I know. I think Donna is setting me up, but not the way Robert thinks."

"Why does she need money, anyway? Aren't they all rich?"

"They're all afraid the inheritance is going to be tied up in courts and eaten up by lawyers because of the family's involvement in Mrs. Priestly's death. Robert needs money to pay off the loan for the restaurant. Victoria needs it to pay off Emerson's lawyers. Donna apparently wants to try to buy back her husband's love. They all need money, and the quickest way to get it might be to steal the jewelry from the estate. The family has to make it look like theft, and I believe you're talking to the scapegoat. While I'm sitting in jail, they'll be fencing diamonds and emeralds."

"What does this have to do with all the attempts on your life?" he asked, as he pulled the truck up across the street from the Priestly estate.

"I don't know."

"And how do we know that the railing giving way like that wasn't another one?"

"That seems like quite a stretch. No one knew I was coming except Robert, and he's the one who almost went over the edge. You know, he said his sister had come to see him the day before. I can't imagine why she'd try to hurt him, but she had the opportunity to tamper with that railing."

"Robert is falling apart at the seams," Cody said softly. "If he knows something that's dangerous to someone else in his family, he may be close to telling, and that might make him a giant threat."

"I didn't think of that," Cassie said.

"Well, he promised he'd have his police friend check it out and let us know." Cody stared over Cassie's head at the looming gingerbread mansion across the street. "Let's get this over with."

IT WAS SO STRANGE COMING back to this house. For months it had been Cassie's home, and yet it held few distinct memories beyond the night she'd gone outside looking to confirm or at least explain what Mrs. Priestly saw through her window.

Was it because Cassie herself wasn't the same person who had lived here? How long had she been gone? A week or so? And yet everything was different and the interval at this house seemed hazy and unreal.

Cody took her hand as they climbed the few steps up to the porch. She rang the bell and they waited. He clanked the door knocker and they waited some more.

"No one's home," she finally said.

"Not even the maid?"

"Robert said his mother fired her."

"Why?"

"To save money."

"Or to get rid of her if she happened to have planted that jewelry on you," he grumbled.

"Either way, it looks like you get your wish. We might as well go home."

As they left the porch, he paused and turned to her. "Feel like living dangerously?"

"Frankly, it seems to me that's all I have been doing lately. I keep expecting someone to try to shoot me."

"Don't say that."

"What do you have in mind?"

"I'd like to see where the old woman thought she saw a murder."

"You mean the fountain in the back?"

"Yes. Maybe we could approach it from the river. There's a path down there, right?"

"Yes, but the gate is latched and sometimes locked, so you wouldn't be able to get back into the garden. There's also a path around the side of the house. I'll knock on the back door just to cover our bases in case Donna or Victoria are hovering out of sight. It's around this way."

She led him through a rusty-looking gate, noting to herself that it didn't appear the gardener was coming around anymore, either.

Cassie knocked on the back door, but this one had a glass panel, and a peek inside revealed the house looked dark and currently unoccupied. She led the way through the garden along the brick path to the fountain and, despite the fact there was absolutely nothing amiss, felt a shudder run through her body.

The big, round fountain was the showpiece of the garden. It was built into a central diamond-shaped area with paths leading away on all four sides. Brick columns located on each corner held lights, although in Cassie's time at the mansion only three had ever worked, and on that last night when she'd come out here in the rain, there'd been no outdoor electricity at all.

Cody took the west path past the fountain and toward the river gate, which he peered through for a minute before returning to her side.

"So this is the fountain?" he said, standing with his hands on his waist and staring at the trio of fish spitting water into the air. "Show me which window was hers, Cass."

Cassie counted one over from the middle of the house, two stories up. "That one."

"How did she get up there?"

"There's an elevator leading to all three floors."

He studied Mrs. Priestly's window again. "That's quite a distance from her window to this fountain."

"Yes. And at night with lousy weather and ninety-three-year-old eyes, it's a stretch to think she witnessed a murder."

"And yet you keep looking up that drowned man they found downriver."

"Yes. This morning I read that they had an ID."

"Who is he?"

"A drug dealer named Bennie Yates."

"From here?"

"It wasn't clear where he's from."

He kneeled down and regarded a loose paver that rested against the foundation of the fountain. Several of the bricks had buckled and cracked over time, and this one was ajar. "Has it always been this way?"

"As long as I've been here, yes."

"I imagine the police looked closely at this area."

"I would think."

He stood again and surveyed the diamond.

"Must have been pretty once," he said, as his gaze swept over the brick light stations and the benches between the paths. "Very symmetrical, isn't it?"

"Very."

"I know how much you like water. Did you spend your evenings out here?"

He asked the question casually; she glanced at his face and saw only regret. They'd come a long way in the past week or so, traveling from blame and anger to a place of compassion. Could it last, or were they always going to be a breath away from saying and doing the wrong thing?

"I loved it out here in the afternoons," she told him,

"but the electricity was wonky, so the lights didn't work all the time. One of them never worked. So, while the late summer evenings were nice, as it began to get darker earlier, it got a little creepy, what with the trail leading down to the river right on the other side of the fence."

He took her hands in his and embraced her. Then he let her go and walked over to the brick column closest to the river. Each of the pillars were about four feet high and two feet square, with an ornate metal cage on top that fit over a light fixture. The sides of the cage were made of brass grillwork, while the top surface itself was solid.

"Is this the broken one you mentioned?" he asked.

"Yes. How did you know?"

"I didn't. There's something sparkly on the ground around the base that caught my attention." As he spoke, he gestured at the ground, and Cassie saw sparkly pieces of glass, or maybe mirror. Cody lifted one edge of the metal grill, and it swung open on a long piano hinge along one side. As Cassie joined him, she could see there was no bulb in the socket.

"What are you looking for?" she asked.

"I don't have the slightest idea." He jiggled the fixture but it was solid.

"The columns must be hollow," she said. "You know, for the wiring. I wonder why no one just replaced the lightbulb."

"Doesn't appear upkeep was big on the Banner list of things to do."

"No, I imagine they'll sell this place as soon as it's theirs to sell." As she spoke she looked at the bricks on the north side more closely. One looked askew, and maybe it was her imagination, but the lichen on that brick looked different than on the adjoining bricks.

"Cody?" she said. "What do you make of this?"

He kneeled down and touched the brick she indicated. They both heard it grate against the others. When he grasped it by the top and bottom edges and pulled, it slipped out in his hand. Attached to the back was an eyebolt, and attached to that was a chain. As he pulled on the chain, he looked up at Cassie. "There's something tied to the end."

"Like a murder weapon? Maybe we should call the police."

"A murder weapon? Oh, you mean for the guy Mrs. Priestly thought she saw murdered. I though you'd given up on that. At any rate, let's see what it is before we call the cops."

"Wait." Cassie dug around in her handbag for a package of tissues. She handed Cody a couple, which he used to keep his fingers from touching any surface that would take a print.

What showed up was a small, brown plastic case that fit through the eleven-by-four-inch hole without much trouble.

Using another tissue, Cassie closed the hinged top of the column, making a flat surface for Cody where he could set the brick and the attached box.

"Maybe there's a gun or a knife inside," she said.

Using the tissues, he opened the two latches.

A large velvet drawstring bag lay inside the box. Cody picked up the bag, again using the tissue, and shook the contents on to the grill.

A dazzling explosion of white light met their gazes. Diamonds galore.

Cody separated the pieces with one of his keys. When he was finished, there were six diamond necklaces and one ring. But the ring was a sparkler with a green sizzle—an emerald the size of a blueberry, set in a floral diamond setting. A ring that Cassie had last seen when she wrapped it in a washcloth and sent it to the Banners.

"That jerk!" Cassie said, her hands balled into fists. "He had it the whole time. And the necklaces, too. Is there anything else in that box?"

"The stub of a pencil and a razor blade," Cody said. "Oh, and a couple of rubber bands, a scrap of paper with nothing on it and another shard of that glass. But we don't know that Emerson put this stuff out here. Any of them could have. It has to be some insurance scam."

"I have a bad feeling about this," Cassie said, glancing at her watch. They'd lingered in the garden for too long and suddenly the windows facing the fountain all seemed like watchful eyes. It was getting late and the autumn light was fading quickly. "We need to leave."

Cody replaced the jewelry in the plastic box, still careful not to touch anything. While he did that, Cassie used more tissues to wipe down the smooth surfaces of the grillwork that they'd touched. "Hurry," she said, looking around fretfully.

"Why? Do you hear something?"

"No." But the word had barely left her lips when her ears picked up the faint, distinctive sound of a tired old motor followed by a banging sound. She'd heard that sound many, many times before.

"That's the garage door opener," she said. "Mrs. Banner must be home."

"Didn't you want to talk to her and Donna?"

"Not like this and not after what we've found. No thanks. I'll think of another way to help Robert."

"Does either woman come outside this time of day?"

"Not often, but Mrs. Banner does tend to go to her

room and change clothes before dinner. Her window is that one right there," Cassie added, pointing at a glass rectangle one floor up and two down from Mrs. Priestly's. "We have to leave."

Cody started to replace the box.

"Wait, what are you doing?"

"I'm putting everything back the way it was."

"No, no, no," she said quickly. "Cody, that box is the only proof we have I didn't mess with the jewelry."

"I know it is. We'll call the police—"

"No. If Mrs. Banner sees us out here when we leave and if she's the one who hid this stuff it'll be gone by the time the police get here."

"We'll stand right here and guard it until they come. We can call Deputy what's-his-name. Tucker." He took out his cell phone.

"Get serious," she said, then jerked as she realized the downstairs lights had switched on. "Tucker thinks I blew up an apartment. He probably thinks I framed Mr. Banner, too, and there's no getting around the fact we're trespassing. I do not want to spend the night in the Cherrydell jail. Let's think of something else."

The garden lights flashed on, catching them both off guard, and they flinched. Many of the shadowed corners were suddenly illuminated, though their area stayed relatively obscure.

"Cody! Please, don't replace that box."

"I won't." He dashed across the diamond to the fountain and grabbed the loose paver. A moment later he knelt down and jabbed it in the hole in the pillar. It wasn't a perfect fit, and if anyone looked, they'd see right away that it had been tampered with.

A new light flickering on in the house caught Cassie's attention. This time what she saw momentarily stopped her heart beating in her chest. Emerson Banner stood framed in the third-story window, and it looked as if he was staring right at her.

She gasped.

Cody must have sensed her panic. He turned to look where her gaze was directed. "Damn," he muttered, and immediately tucked the box and the brick attached to it under his arm and grabbed Cassie's hand. They didn't exchange a word, just made for the river gate. A moment later, they'd unlatched it and exited the property.

Cassie caught sight of a walker coming along the bank from the East. There were seldom people out here on a cold afternoon, and she was surprised. She couldn't make out who it was; hopefully, if she couldn't see his face, he couldn't see hers. She tugged on Cody's hand, pointed at the walker and they took off.

"This way," she whispered, and they headed down toward the river, angling west, moving along the path as quickly as they dared. But they didn't make it far until Cassie, who was in front, tripped over something and started to fall.

Cody caught her.

"What is it?" he said, but at the same instant, they both realized exactly what "it" was.

A body lay across the path.

At the realization of what had tripped her Cassie wasn't sure if she was going to throw up or faint. She sank abruptly to the top of a large rock as Cody knelt to check.

"Is he—"

"Dead? Very. Maybe a day or so. Looks like half his head is caved in."

"Do you know who it is?"

"Never seen him.

Cassie steeled herself for a glance.

What was left of the man's face belonged to a stranger. He had dark hair and was wearing jeans, running shoes and a jacket.

One arm extended toward the river which was about ten feet away. The other lay palm upward, above his head. The jacket sleeve had ridden up his arm, revealing his wrist. In the fading light, Cassie could just make out a tattoo of a heart filled with the letters D C.

She took a shallow breath, very aware of the smell of death. "I think it's Kevin Cooke, Donna's husband."

"What's that bulge under his jacket?" Cody asked.

"Where?"

He picked up a stick and lifted the hem to reveal a gun jammed in the waistband of the dead man's jeans. Just about all that showed of it was the ivory white grip. "What do you want to bet that belongs to Emerson Banner?" Cody said, letting the jacket fall back into place. "We have to call the cops."

She shook her head. "No."

"There's no choice—"

"We're standing here with stolen property," she reminded him, nodding at the box still tucked under his arm, "next to a man who it appears has been trying to kill me. Look at those shoes—Sally saw shoes just like them. This is the gunman. Let's call the murder in anonymously. No one knows we're here."

"Are you forgetting Banner?"

"If he'd seen us he would have come after us. No one knows…."

They looked at each other as her voice trailed off. Suddenly, they were both standing. Cassie had just flashed on the walker they'd seen a few minutes before and judging by the way Cody's gaze darted up the hazy trail, so had he.

"Time to leave," he said, throwing the stick into the river.

He got no argument from her.

Chapter Fifteen

They stopped briefly at a pay phone to leave an anonymous call about their grisly find, then drove as fast as they dared, making straight for the Wyoming border.

"I wonder how many laws we broke today," Cassie said through chattering teeth. The chills had started the second they reached the relative safety of the truck, and though she'd turned the heater on full blast, she was still freezing.

Plus, she was crampy and uncomfortable. *Great.*

"Better not to think about it. You know what this means, right? If Kevin Cooke was the one shooting at you, and it appears he must have been, then it's over."

"He must have been in cahoots with Donna. Who knows how much more she stole from her grandmother that's still undiscovered? She and her husband must have assumed I was aware of a lot more than I actually was. He may even have killed Mrs. Priestly to try to cover their tracks."

"It's funny that you never met him, isn't it? If she was over at the Priestly house so often, it seems you would have at least seen him."

"Not really. Donna visited during the day while her husband worked. Mrs. Priestly folded up camp pretty early in the evening. And more than that, Donna's parents didn't really like Kevin."

"I wonder where he's been since her death."

"Running around shooting at me and my friends," she said dryly. "Messing with lug nuts. Making my life hell. What I wonder is who killed him and why. Banner is out on bail—maybe he did the dirty deed."

"That guy was dead before Banner made bail. My money is on Donna. And I think Robert knew something was going on with his sister and that's why he's been falling apart. She must have rigged his railing, hoping to get rid of him, and he probably knows that, too, even if he doesn't want to think about it."

Cassie rubbed her side and tried to relax. "Right now, I don't care who did what to who as long as no one is coming after me," she said, and she meant it.

"Are you okay?"

"Just a twinge. The last week or so is catching up with me."

"Tomorrow I'm supposed to help with the cattle," he said. "I can't imagine leaving you."

"It won't take you more than a few hours, and I'll have Mike and Echo and Pauline to help me. You have to go. Pierce isn't here and Mike is injured. I plan on laying real low."

"We'll see," he said.

"We still have that box to deal with."

"I'm calling our attorney, like I should have done a week ago, and asking him to come out to the house tomorrow night. For now, I'll lock it in our safe. We're going to let him figure out how to get it to the right authorities. There's going to be a lot to deal with in the coming weeks and we need guidance. Time to stop hiding. That okay with you?"

"Not really, but there's no choice, I know that." She smothered a yawn and laid her head back against the rest.

"The twinges gone?"

"Mostly."

He was quiet for a second, trying to figure out how to broach what he wanted to say. As usual, it subtly evaded him—might just as well say it. "I know making love doesn't solve everything," he began.

"I'm glad to hear you say that," she said.

He hadn't been finished. He'd been about to add a *but*. Now he said, "Why?"

"Well, you know, we've always been attracted to each other. I bet we could be apart fifty years and still get the hots for each other."

"That's probably true, but I don't want us to be apart fifty years, do you?"

"No," she said, but she didn't sound very convincing.

He was incredulous, like a man is when he struggles to reach a mountain peak only to get knocked down by an avalanche a foot from the summit.

"We made a deal back on day one," she added, sparing him a glance. "We would get our baby safely into the world and then decide about our future because no matter what happened last night, the fact remains you are in this unwillingly. There's no way to change that. Can't we just stick with our original plan?"

"Even if we outgrow it?"

"Let's just see what happens. Nothing is written in stone, not for me, and not for you. Contrary to what you said, a baby doesn't take away your options. Only you can do that."

She was giving him a ticket out of their marriage. And she thought she was doing him a favor.

THEY ARRIVED HOME to find the ranch covered in an inch of snow, with no signs of the snowfall letting up. The outbuildings were all brightly lit.

Adam greeted them as he crossed the yard. "We're headed out bright and early," he called. He carried a saddle on one shoulder while snowflakes swirled around his head. "Pierce phoned. He and Analise are in New York. They'll be home tomorrow."

"Why aren't we waiting for him?" Cody asked.

"You know Dad," Adam said. "Claims we've waited long enough as it is. Dennis Garvey signed on to go with us. We'll be fine."

"Okay. I'm going inside with Cass to take care of something. I'll come help in a few minutes."

"Sounds good," Adam said, and walked off.

They had agreed not to mention Kevin Cooke's body or their role in finding it. Things would come out in the end, but right now neither one of them wanted to involve their family in their complicity.

Pauline and Echo looked up as they walked through the kitchen. The two women were in the process of baking pasties, handheld savory pies that were Birch's favorites when he hit the trail. The smell of simmering meat and vegetables perfumed the air. Even Bonnie couldn't be bothered with more than a cursory wag-of-the-tail greeting as she quietly begged from her blanket.

Once again, Cody locked the office door behind them and moved directly to the safe. He set the brick and the brown box on the desktop, then turned to the painting of the old hunting lodge and swung it away from the wall.

Cassie watched as he opened the safe. For a few seconds, he just stood there staring into it, and then he reached in and took something before turning back to her.

His expression was impossible to read, but his gaze seemed to drill right into her head. He walked back to stand in front of her, then invited her to sit. She chose the same chair she had the night before.

"I have something for you," he said softly.

Oh, dear Lord, she suddenly knew what was coming.

He stood over her, staring down at her, his dark eyes tender and hard at the same time.

"Let me tell you something," he began, his right hand in a fist. "A few days after you left I went to Woodwind and checked every hotel. I finally found the one you stayed at. It was part of a chain. The woman there told me you'd come into the office and taken maps for Idaho and that you'd made a reservation in Boise and then you'd driven off.

"That's when I knew you'd really left me. I drove to Boise, but you weren't there. I hired a detective."

"I know most of this," she said gently. It was terrible to witness his pain. She didn't tell him she'd made that reservation as a ruse, as she'd been pretty sure he'd do exactly as he'd done. She didn't tell him she'd actually driven to Washington state before making her way back to Idaho. She'd needed time to think....

"So, now I'll tell you something you don't know. When I got back to Woodwind, I went into the best jewelry store in town and told them what I wanted. A week later, they called and I went to pick it up. My plan was to put it on your finger the minute I found you."

He sat on the chair next to hers and opened his hand, revealing the ring box she'd last seen in his duffel bag.

"Why didn't you do it the way you planned?" she

whispered. Her throat was choked with raw emotion as his dark eyes searched her face.

"Because there were other factors."

"The baby."

"Yes, the baby. But there was also you and me." He took a deep, shuddering breath. "I hadn't thought things through. I hadn't realized I'd be angry with you when I found you or that you'd be angry with me. And every day that passed made giving this to you harder because of our deal."

"Why now?" she murmured.

He opened the box and the sparkle of the diamonds and emeralds glowed in its velvet cradle.

"Tonight I realized I've been looking at this all wrong," he said. "That we've been looking at it wrong. People are either committed to one another or they're not. You can't play games with that kind of thing. And no matter what you decide in the end, my mind is already made up. I'm a one-woman man, Cassie, and you're my woman. I bought this as a symbol of forever. I know it doesn't look like much next to that whopper in the box over there, but this one is yours."

He took the ring out of the box and offered it to her. "You said nothing is written in stone," he mumbled. "I guess that's true. But I know how I feel. I just wish I was better with words."

He'd taken her hand as he spoke and now slid the ring on her finger where it nestled against her wedding band. It looked as though it had been there from day one.

She looked from it to Cody as tears slid down her cheeks. "For a man not good with words, you're doing a pretty good job," she said. Her breath caught as he gathered her in his arms and kissed her.

THEY RODE OUT BEFORE daylight. There were five of them:
Birch, Adam, Cody, Jamie and Uncle Pete. Because of
his sore back, Mike had had to stay behind, and Dennis
Garvey hadn't shown up as promised. Cody knew Dennis's no-show was a big disappointment to Adam, who
appeared determined to help the kid whether he wanted
it or not.

And wasn't that just the way it was? Here was Adam
all ready to assume responsibility for a sixteen-year-old
boy while most of the time, Cody couldn't even manage
to think about a six- or seven-pound newborn baby.

A few inches of snow had accumulated during the
night, and it continued snowing as they rode across
Open Sky land. Cody was torn about leaving Cassie's
side, though his honesty made him admit it felt great to
be astride Bandido, off to round up a part of the herd and
drive them home. It seemed forever since he'd worked
at being what he really was—a cowboy.

This role came easier than husband and potential
father, but was that so terrible? Didn't everybody wear
several hats in their lives, and weren't some bound to
be more comfortable?

He'd given Mike strict orders to stay close to the
house. It seemed unlikely any of the Banners would
show up. They were undoubtedly swamped with police
and questions and death today. Just the same, Mike had
his orders.

It took a couple of hours for the five men to get up
to the Hayfork pasture, and that was using the quickest
trail, one which was too steep and narrow to drive the
cattle along for the return trip. For that, they would need
to take the easier route, which meant they had to cross
the highway about two miles from the ranch. That was

the major reason they needed a good contingency of men and horses to manage the situation.

The rest of the men—and Dennis—had spent the day before getting the cattle grouped in the lower part of the pasture. As they approached now, Cody could hear the lowing of the herd, a sound that never failed to rouse him.

The next couple of hours were spent directing the herd in the right direction. Jamie and Birch rode point while Adam and Pete worked the back, crisscrossing each other as they applied steady pressure to move forward. Uncle Pete, a little rustier than the rest of them, rode on ahead.

It was dirty work. All those hooves churning the new snow made mud, and half that mud seemed to get kicked back onto Adam and Cody, where it mixed with the falling flakes and made a cold, glorious mess.

CASSIE WANDERED AROUND the house, unconsciously rubbing her stomach. The twinges she'd first experienced on their trip home from Cherrydell were back.

Pauline wasn't in the kitchen, which meant she was probably in her own room taking a well-deserved break. Echo had said she'd come over to stay with Cassie toward noon. Even Bonnie was outside, presumably with Mike. It was strangely quiet in the house, and a little isolated.

The baby was relatively still, but occasionally Cassie felt a faint flutter, and that served as a reminder she soon would have little time to feel lonesome. Still restless, she wandered into the living room and built up the fire. She admired the tree and the falling snow outside the window, but she wound up in the office, which had become one of her favorite rooms since her return.

The furniture was big and masculine and there was too much of it, but it was also a smallish room compared to the rest of the house, with one window looking over the mountains and a door that closed. There was a feeling of security in this room the rest of the rambling log house couldn't duplicate.

She chose her favorite wing chair and sat down with a sigh. The light sparkled on the diamonds of the ring Cody had given her the night before, and she smiled as she recalled everything he said when he gave it to her.

No, these stones weren't as big as the Priestly emerald. And the diamonds weren't as brilliant white, either. So what?

And yet the Wild Iris didn't fool around with lesser-quality stones.

Curious now, she went to the safe and opened it. Before she touched the box and the brick to which it was still attached, she fetched her gloves from the coat closet and put them on, then hurried back into the den.

The diamonds were all but blinding in the reflection of the desk light. It was the emerald she was after, though, and once again she marveled at the size and the clarity of the central stone. Holding her ring next to it, she was stunned at the difference between her stones and the Priestly emerald.

She dug around in the desk drawer until she found the powerful magnifying glass Cody had kept from the days he collected stamps as a kid, and she looked at her stones.

Each was a lovely grass-green color, although one was a little murkier than the others, and all had tiny irregular patterns or flaws. Then she looked through the magnifying glass at the Priestly emerald. Not a single imperfection.

Didn't all natural stones have flaws?

Was the Priestly emerald a fake? Was that possible?

She set the ring down and picked up one of the diamond necklaces and looked at it through the glass, too, and this time her heart kind of accelerated.

These were supposed to be top-quality diamonds set in platinum, and yet the metal appeared to be tarnished. Platinum doesn't tarnish, even she knew that. And the diamonds themselves, those beautiful crystal-white stones, why, they were absolutely flawless, each and every one of them.

There was a glass blotter on the desktop. She chose the largest Priestly diamond and dragged it sharply across the surface. Then she angled her own ring and did the same with one of the diamonds....

Diamonds are harder than glass. Hers left a scratch. The Priestly gem, twenty times as big, didn't make a mark.

She sat back in the chair and stared at the pile of glitter. She felt pretty sure she was looking at a whole lot of crystal and maybe sterling silver....

There was no way to know for absolute sure, not without a jeweler testing the stones, but she would be willing to bet the whole lot were fakes.

So, it appeared Donna and her husband had been taking the jewelry, replacing the real stones with fakes.

As she put it all back into the brown box, she noticed the other bits and pieces Cody had mentioned. The pencil and paper, shard of glass and rubber band—the kind of things that seem to always turn up in old boxes and drawers.

They would return all this to the police via their lawyer. The Banners would no doubt claim she and Cody switched the jewels, but a good investigator would discover the real culprit.

The office computer sprang to life at a touch and she researched fake gemstones versus real ones for a few minutes until she realized she'd done all she could for now. She checked out Kevin Cooke next and read an article in the Cherrydell newspaper about an anonymous tip uncovering the murder of a local businessman. There were few details pending investigation, but there was a picture of Kevin taken sometime earlier with Donna at his side.

They looked happy.

Then, more or less out of habit, she typed in the drowning victim, using his name this time—Bennie Yates.

The newest article came with an old photo taken a year before.

He looked familiar.

She stared at the blurry head shot as her mind immediately skipped to the report of the snake tattoos. There was something reptilian about the man's features. A small head, slicked-back hair, flat nose, eyes a trifle slanted and oddly colorless...

Okay, this was giving her the creeps. She'd seen this man somewhere...

With shaking hands, she opened the safe again, fumbling the lock before finally yanking the door open. This time she snatched the box without thinking about gloves and fingerprints. She dumped out the jewelry and stared down at the old razor blade.

At the piece of glass. No, not glass, mirror. She kept thinking of it as glass because it was so small. But there had been a fragment of the same material on the ground at the base of the pillar, too.

A razor and a mirror, a drug dealer named Bennie Yates and a riverside hidey-hole—

Cassie grabbed the phone, her intention to call the Cherrydell Police Department. The line was silent. The phone must be off the hook somewhere else in the house....

She heard a noise outside the office. Chills splattered her skin like cold drops of rain as the door slowly opened.

Chapter Sixteen

It took a long time to move the animals down the slopes to the meadow. When they were close enough, Cody and Adam rode ahead to open the gates on either side of the two-lane highway.

Even though Open Sky land was only two miles away, that was by highway and they couldn't drive the animals down the road. The path would be three times as long.

Cody was dismayed to find steady traffic. The weather wasn't as bad down at this elevation and people were out and about.

Adam got off Solar Flare as they both became aware of a horseman galloping toward them on the shoulder of the road. As he got closer, they discovered it was Dennis Garvey.

He was dressed in a bulky jacket against the cold, and it made him appear twice as big as he really was. But there was color in his thin face for a change, and he had a coil of rope tied to his saddle.

"You're late," Adam said, as he rolled back the wood-framed barbed-wire fence onto itself to form a gate. "I don't have much need for a man who doesn't show up when he says he will."

To his credit, Dennis got off his mount and tied the

horse to a post. He tugged on leather gloves and gave Adam a hand with the fence. Cody paused to hear what excuse the boy would come up with for his tardiness.

"They let Tommy out of rehab last night," Dennis said. "He's back at the house expecting me to take care of him until his trial. I wasn't sure what to do 'bout this morning."

"So you blew us off."

"I guess. Then Tommy wanted me to go buy him beer using his ID, and he started making fun of me working with you guys and saying I had to do what he said 'cause he was boss. I've had it with him. If you're willing to give me another chance, I'd sure like to take it."

Adam made a show of thinking about it. "You get on that horse and ride back there and help keep the herd in one spot while we finish getting the fences ready."

"Yes, sir," Dennis said, and was back on his horse and trotting away before they knew it.

"You're going to make a good dad," Cody said.

"So are you if you ever stop being an idiot," Adam said, but the words were delivered with a grin.

Cody moved across the road and uncoiled the opposite fence, then started back to the herd he could see was a quarter mile up the meadow and coming fast toward the first gate.

Dennis turned out to be a pretty good horseman, which came as a surprise to nobody but Cody as the others had all worked with him the day before. They moved the cattle toward the fence, keeping two riders in front.

Cody waited for a long gap in the traffic, then he and Uncle Pete rode out onto the road. Still astride their mounts, they brought the north-south traffic to a standstill while the others guided the herd through the makeshift corridor.

Everything would have been okay if some impatient jerk a car or two back hadn't honked his horn. It spooked one of the cows, who jumped out of the pack and tore off down the verge next to the fence.

The rest of the herd picked up on the renegade's escape. There were a few anxious minutes keeping the rest from making a break for it. At last Cody was able to signal Adam his intention to go after the stray, turning Bandido just in time to see Dennis take off.

An oath of frustration died on Cody's lips as the kid produced a lasso while riding lickety-split. He put the rope around the animal's head and brought it under control just about as slick as anyone could want.

As the herd disappeared safely up the slope beyond the fence, Cody rode off to help Dennis. They straddled the cow, who, feeling the presence of the two horses and men on either side, continued to calm down. "Good thing you showed up," Cody told the boy.

"Yeah. I wasn't sure what to do when I went by the ranch and everything was all closed up, but then I remembered Adam saying you guys planned to cross the highway and I figured you'd need help."

"Wait," Cody said. "What do you mean everything was all closed up? Mike was there, and Cassie and Pauline and the dog—"

"I didn't see no one and I never heard no dog."

"Oh, God," Cody said, imagining the most obvious scenario. Cassie had gone into labor and they'd all rushed her to the hospital.

Without calling him?

But there was another possibility. Donna Cooke seeking revenge…

As the boy released the lasso and swatted the cow on the rump to send it back to the herd, Cody made a decision. "Put that fence back together. Make sure you do a good job. Then tell Adam what you just told me about the ranch. I'm going back the fastest way, and that's the way you came. I'm counting on you, Dennis."

And before the kid could respond, Cody took off down the side of the highway, his heart beating in time with the thunder of Bandido's hooves against the earth.

Eventually he calmed down enough to use his head, and slowing the horse, took out his cell phone and called the ranch. The line was busy, and when it switched to call waiting he left a hurried message. He tried the hospital next, but Cassie hadn't been admitted. She could have been in transit. He called Echo at Adam's house, and she answered immediately.

"I was just on my way out the door," she said. "I'm going over to stay with Cassie."

"Then you haven't heard from her? I can't reach her, and Dennis Garvey said the ranch looked deserted."

"I haven't heard a word. I'll hurry over."

"No," he said. "I'm not far away. Call the sheriff, get him over there, but you stay home."

"Why? She may need help."

"Mike is there and Pauline. I can't imagine why they haven't called you unless there's some kind of trouble. Just keep trying to contact Cass, but don't go to the main house unless she tells you it's okay. You don't want to walk into a trap. I've got to go."

He stuck the phone back in his pocket and urged Bandido forward. A few minutes later, he approached the ranch from the top of the hill and paused, looking for some sign of turmoil.

From this vantage point, he could see Adam's truck

right where he'd parked it the night before. Pauline's car was pulled around near her room in the back, as it usually was. There was no sign of Bonnie and none of Mike, nor could he see a vehicle that didn't belong at the ranch.

He took a fast but circuitous route, taking cover behind the first building he came to, which happened to be the maintenance barn. His plan was to leave Bandido tied up inside and go on alone. There were huge rolling doors on the opposite end of the building to allow tractor access, but he chose a small side entrance. It came as a surprise when he found the big doors wide open.

A hay truck had been pulled toward that front, facing out as though in the process of leaving. A black sedan with Idaho plates was parked in front of it at an angle.

Banner!

No sooner had he seen the car than he heard a dog whining. He looped Bandido's reins around the bumper of the hay truck, grabbed his rifle and hurried toward the sound, which was very close by.

He found Bonnie standing in the space between the hay truck and the car. She moved away when he tried to touch her, trotting around toward the front of the building until she stopped by a prone shape. She sat down as if guarding it.

Mike. Lying on his back. Rigid and deathly still, but alive.

He was at Mike's side in a second, kneeling on the dirt floor. The ranch hand had been shot in the leg, but there wasn't a lot of blood, at least not enough to support the horrific way his face contorted in pain.

No need to ask what had happened. Banner had driven into the barn and attacked when Mike challenged him. Cody stripped off his coat and covered Mike. "Where's Cassie and Pauline?"

"I don't know," Mike said through gritted teeth, as additional beads of sweat popped out on his pale forehead. His breaths were shallow and gasping.

"Are you hit somewhere besides your leg?" Cody asked as he took out his phone.

"No. Back spasm. Bastard shot me. My back went out when I jerked. Can't move. Can't hardly breathe."

"I'll leave the phone," Cody said, folding it in Mike's hand. "How many?"

"One."

Bonnie lay down beside Mike as Cody ran toward the doors. Why hadn't he brought Adam?

There were plenty of structures between the barn and the house, which was about twelve hundred feet away. Cody took advantage of each. As he darted between buildings he considered the best way to enter the house and decided on Pauline's room. It was located in the rear, and a stranger probably wouldn't think of guarding it like they might a front or back door.

He knew their housekeeper liked to sleep with an open window no matter what the weather, and much to his relief, he found it unlatched. Carefully, he slid the casing up and pulled himself into the room.

Pauline lay across the bed as though she'd fallen there, the telephone receiver in her hand. A knot the size of a golf ball and a mass of oozing flesh on the back of her head explained her unconscious condition and brought back a vivid image of Kevin Cooke's bashed-in skull. The wound looked relatively fresh. Cody paused to check her breathing.

Her eyelids fluttered open. She looked confused. "Ssh," Cody told her, taking the phone out of her hands.

"Don't replace it on the cradle," he said, afraid it would ring and alert the intruder that someone else was inside. "Are you okay for a few minutes?"

"Where's Cassie?"

"I don't know," he said. He shifted the rifle to his other hand. "I'll take care of her. You stay here."

"Hurry, before it's too late."

CASSIE STARED AT THE MAN in her doorway with a sense of inevitability she couldn't deny. She should have known all along—maybe she had.

"So, you found my stash," Robert said, as he stepped across the threshold into the office and gestured at the heap of fake diamonds.

Her gaze traveled from the gun in his hand to his wild eyes. He was coming unglued from the inside out, had been for days, maybe weeks, and now she was pretty sure she understood why. It wasn't his family falling apart or fear for his business. It wasn't his sister or his brother-in-law or anyone else.

"I saw you come out of the garden last night," he said. "I knew you and Cody had snooped around and discovered my secret."

"We discovered something else, too," she said softly.

"Ah, and isn't it ironic that you should have been the one to come across Kevin. What an imbecile." His free hand twitched at his side. "He ran off with some stripper and then she ran off with someone else. He came to me to help him get back into Donna's good graces."

"So you took him over to the mansion and instead of acting as a mediator, bashed him over the head and planted your father's gun on him to make him the scape-goat. Was that before or after you shot at Sally?"

"After, obviously," he said. "But I didn't know I'd hit

the wrong person until I called here to make sure you were dead and you answered the phone." He laughed too loud and too long, then clamped his mouth shut and rubbed his eyes with his free hand. As he walked closer, waves of tension crackled the air around him. He was so wired his voice vibrated with anxiety. "So, did you figure it *all* out?"

"I think so. Your grandmother saw you kill Bennie Yates, didn't she? You dumped him in the river, then ran back inside and came out again pretending to help me."

"Detective Taipan, as you knew him, got a little impatient when I couldn't pay what I owed him."

"You bankrupted your restaurant, tapped out your father, stole jewels from your grandmother, all to finance a drug habit," Cassie said. "Bennie was your supplier. You rigged the lights in your parents' garden and used the pillar as a drop site. You'd leave money, Bennie would leave drugs."

"Except for the one time he came to my restaurant to threaten me and you ran into him."

"He was on his way to the private exit at the end of the hall. He gripped my arms when we collided and I saw a wavy stripe on his hand that barely registered in my brain. It was a serpent's tongue, wasn't it?"

Robert waved the gun like it was an extension of his hand. "Stupid tattoos. Even the name he gave you was a tip-off. Taipan, the most deadly snake in the world. Nasty buggers, but Bennie had a thing for them. Anyway, when you told me you'd met him outside my office I knew you had to go. Sooner or later Bennie's body would show up and there was too good a chance you'd recognize a photograph."

"And yet you failed to kill me over and over again."

"Let's hope practice makes perfect," he said.

She'd had some of it right, just with the wrong person. "You've been clever," she said, fighting to keep her voice steady and calm. "You must be dying to talk about it. I bet you've been taking your grandmother's diamonds for years and replacing the stones with fake ones. Any missing jewels discovered during the audit would be assumed to be as real as the ones you made sure it looked like I pilfered. It all fits except for the phony emerald ring."

"A little mistake on my part," Robert said. His eyes truly were too bright, like he was high on something. That could explain the braggart quality to his voice. Cassie wondered if this all seemed like a dream to him.

"The emerald ring was the only colored stone I switched. I meant to hide it in the box with the necklaces but I put it in your purse instead. Coincidentally, I'd driven straight home after you survived my first attack up on that hill. When I saw your package in the morning mail I couldn't believe my luck."

"So you opened it before your parents did and took out the ring."

"And stuck it in with the fake diamonds. Exactly."

"So that's why you didn't care if the jewels got blown up with me when you rigged the heater at the apartment. You wanted that ring destroyed. How did you know I was there?"

"Your husband led me right to you. After he left, I waited until the wake was long over and my parents had gone out to eat, then I went back to your apartment and created a gas leak. The owner had an extra garage door opener hanging on the wall so I swiped it and hid out down the block."

"That was the clicking sound we heard. When you

saw us coming out of the apartment earlier than you expected, you hit the switch and it caused a spark."

Robert opened his hand fast, as though emulating an explosion and grinned at her. "It should have worked perfectly. And it would have, except for your husband. He's there every time, isn't he, looking after you, protecting you?"

She glanced down at her ring finger. "Yes," she murmured and in that moment understood that she and Cody's future *was* written in stone—these stones. These symbols of how he felt in his heart despite the fears and uncertainties.

Real stones, real meanings... "Yes," she murmured. "He's been there for me every time."

Robert laughed again. "Except now. Too bad." Scowling, he turned serious. "Come out from behind the desk."

She wrapped her arms around her middle as she moved into the room as directed. Was she trying to protect her baby, or was she hoping the sight of her would awaken the humanity in Robert? Both notions seemed unlikely.

"I liked you," he said suddenly. "I never intended—"

"You never intended to have to look me in the eye when you murdered me. Is that what you want to say?"

"Yesterday—"

"The railing? You were trying to throw me off that deck, weren't you?"

He nodded.

She swallowed what felt like a brick of air. "Listen to me, Robert. You kill me and you kill this child. My heart stops beating and his or her heart stops, too. Are you prepared to do such a thing?"

"Yes," he said, but the gun barrel actually lowered a hair, and his hand shook. Other than the rigged railing, every attempt on her life had been from a distance. Both her shooting and Sally's were done so far away they were failures. Tampering with the lug nuts on the wheel was relatively impersonal. So was the explosion at the apartment. Hopefully he didn't have the guts to look her in the eye—

He'd killed Kevin Cooke up close and personal.

Sensing movement, she glanced over Robert's shoulder in time to see something small and round appear in the open door behind him. The barrel of a rifle! Just as hope surged through her body, Robert grabbed her wrist and pulled her close. He jabbed the muzzle under her chin.

"I think I'm over being squeamish," he said.

Cassie had to stall him. That had to be Mike out there in the hall, she had to give him a chance.

"Listen, no one but me knows about Bennie—"

"Are you trying to tell me you won't tell anyone? Do you think I'd believe that? Maybe my mother keeps quiet, but why should you?"

"Your mother followed you that night, didn't she? That's why she was outside."

"She was suspicious. She saw me hit Bennie. I told her killing him was an accident and we had to get rid of his body. She believed me because she wanted to."

"But don't you see?" Cassie continued. "You can convince others that it was an accident, too. You're an upstanding citizen from a good family. Bennie was a drug dealer who corrupted who knows how many people up and down that river."

"You're forgetting Kevin."

"No, I'm not. Who's to question if his death was murder or self defense? You don't have a record, it's not like you've hurt anyone else."

"No," he said, almost dreamily. "No one else."

At the weird tone of his voice, she twisted her head to look up at him. He stared right into her eyes and she knew.

"The day after you killed your drug supplier, your grandmother looked out in the garden and gasped," she whispered. "I wondered what had alarmed her so I looked, too. Your parents were out there with the judge and lawyer. I thought their presence frightened her. But it wasn't them she was worried about, was it? You were there, too, standing by the fountain."

"Why would she be worried about me?" he said, but she could feel his body tense.

"Because that's the moment she began to suspect it was you she'd seen out in the garden, isn't it?"

"You're not making sense," he said. "If she suspected I was a murderer then she would have written me out of her will that day. She had the lawyer right there, she took Dad out and put you in, but she left me alone."

"She *wouldn't* write you out of her will because she loved you. She wanted to punish your father, but not you. She loved you."

One tear rolled down Robert's newly gaunt cheek. "The fake diamonds were still in her room," he said in a voice that seemed to float away. "Dad confided he was being audited, and the household belongings would be included because Grandma was certain some of her things were missing or different... I had to get those necklaces back."

"Why didn't you just walk in and take them?"

"Because she wouldn't leave her room. I didn't have a choice. Things were happening too fast. And anyway, it had to look like an outside job. I had it all figured out..."

"So you climbed up a ladder and came through her window."

"She should have slept through it."

"But she didn't."

"She woke up and saw me and she knew *everything*. She pointed her finger at me. She said I had until morning to tell the police or she would. I…I panicked."

"And smothered her with her own pillow," Cassie cried. "A frail, elderly woman whose only weakness was not seeing what a monster you really were!"

Robert pushed Cassie away as though touching her burned his skin. "Shut up," he screamed, the gun in his shaking hand pointed straight at her heart, the heel of his free hand pressed against his temple. "Please, please shut up."

Cassie stumbled backward toward the door, appalled at the crazy light in Robert's eyes. She'd so forgotten everything in her disgust of him, it actually came as a surprise to feel other hands grab her and pull her from the room. So quickly she barely knew what happened, she was swept out of harm's way.

She looked up at her savior and into Cody's eyes. Cody! Of course it was him. It was always him and it always would be.

He turned back to the office. "Give it up, Robert," Cody said, advancing forward, the rifle trained on Robert, Cassie behind him. "Set the gun down on the desk and move away from it."

She was watching as Robert lifted the gun from where it dangled by his side. He paused, looked right into Cassie's eyes, then turned the weapon on himself.

"No!" Cassie screamed as a gunshot blasted the air and Robert seemed to disappear in a red haze. She squeezed her eyes shut to block out the horrific image.

Cody clutched her tightly against his chest and together, they stumbled out of the office.

They looked up as the front door flew open and Adam raced inside.

"I heard a shot," Adam said, coming to a halt. "What happened?"

Cassie tucked herself as close to Cody as she could. Let him explain. She didn't have the heart.

Chapter Seventeen

Over two weeks later, on the day after Thanksgiving and the day before Cassie's baby was due, the whole family and a few good friends assembled in the Open Sky living room for three weddings.

The grooms stood by the fireplace—Birch Westin and his two sons, all tough, strong men, men who reflected the rugged land and lifestyle of their birthplace: this ranch. Cody was acting as best man for his two brothers, and he stood beside them. While Adam and Pierce both looked amazing, it was Cody Cassie's gaze strayed to over and over again.

Cody, with his dark eyes and square shoulders and the way he had of looking at her, half shy, half possessive, one hundred percent smoldering.

Her Cody, whom she'd come so close to losing.

The brides were clustered behind the Christmas tree. Princess Analise was dressed the least formally and yet, true to her station and nature, she looked the most regal. She was dressed in a snow-white sheath with a delicate tiara nestled in her black hair to hold her veil in place. It struck Cassie every time she saw Analise that here was a woman who knew what—and whom—she wanted.

And she wanted Pierce. The sparks between them were palpable.

Then there was Pauline, who just that morning had taken the bandage off her head for the first time. She wore the fanciest dress of all, a light pink frill-fest that reflected the excited blush on her cheeks as she made ready to claim the man she'd served—and loved—for almost thirty years.

Echo, catching sight of Cassie's over-the-shoulder glance, winked. Her dress was also white, but it was lacy and long and fit like a second skin. Echo wore it the way she wore everything—with panache and attitude. She looked like the bride figure atop a wedding cake. And Cassie happened to know she was a month pregnant.

Cassie smiled as she tried to get comfortable on the folding chair. She had a secret of her own.

She'd been having contractions for the past several hours. Nothing too bad yet, nothing that would cause her to delay these weddings, but it wouldn't be long now...

She wiggled on the chair again. The baby took up a lot of her midsection, leaving her wondering if her organs would ever find their way back to their appropriate places after she gave birth.

And just like that, another contraction started but this time it was different.

Now?

The music started. The brides began walking down the makeshift aisle.

Sally wasn't here. She and Ethan had eloped as soon as Sally got out of the hospital, so there was no quiet way to enlist help. Cassie would have to wait this out....

Another contraction shook her and she tried breathing slowly. It took hours to have a baby, especially a first baby. Days even. Weeks, months! She was not going to ruin these fairy-tale weddings. Each and every one of these couples had struggled to make it to this day. She would sit here and get through this, and then she would have a baby while everyone else ate cake.

She gasped into her hand and felt light-headed.

Her gaze darted around all the brides, grooms and the preacher to settle on Cody. He was paying attention to the ceremony, as well he should. She grasped her stomach as delicately as she could and concentrated on breathing.

Think of something else, she told herself. Like Donna Banner. Poor Donna. Her husband dead. Her father back in jail due to parole violation. He'd tried to fly to Cape Verde, where there was no extradition, but he didn't make it past the airport in Boise. Her mother accused of accessory to murder for her part in covering up Bennie Yates's killing. Robert gone. Even worse, he'd killed their grandmother.

Cassie had called Donna to offer condolences and to assure her she didn't want a penny of Mrs. Priestly's money. Donna had dismissed that idea at once. "No way. Grandma loved you, and you were the only one in that house who cared about her for who she was and not what she could do for you. I am so glad she had you the last few months. I'm sorry for everything I said to you."

So Cassie was going to be wealthy in her own right if she didn't pop open and die in the next few minutes.

Because brother, that was how it felt. She knew giving birth was work, she'd read all the books, she'd watched the farm animals do it—but, boy, they made it look easier than this.

She needed to stand up and walk, but she knew the minute she got to her feet all eyes would turn toward her. Why hadn't she left the room when she could?

They were exchanging vows. It took forever! Then

the room grew quiet except for a chorus of masculine *I dos*...

Hurry.

The preacher was talking again. Cassie felt something wet between her legs. Was that her water breaking? Good heavens.

Hurry...

And then she heard the women say *I do,* one after the other, each voice clear and joyful. Cassie sat there as another contraction sucker punched her. Were they supposed to come this fast and furious? Uh-oh...

Cody asked everyone to be quiet. He looked at Cassie and she did her best to plaster on a grin instead of a grimace...

"As long as you're all here, I'd like to ask my wife Cassie to marry me all over again. How about it, Cass? Right now, before the baby, before anything else. Will you marry me? Again?"

Every person in the room was staring at her. The contraction had lessened to the point where she could stand by gripping the back of the chair in front of her and she got to her feet. Water rushed down her legs and puddled on the floor. The man sitting next to her made a startled sound.

It was Echo whose smile turned to alarm.

"Cassie?" she called. "Are you in labor?"

Cassie, touched by Cody's words, overwhelmed with what was happening and truth be told, a little scared, managed a nod.

CODY STOOD ON THE DECK outside and stared at the road, Bonnie standing by his legs.

Where was that damn doctor?

Echo was going to deliver his baby and she'd never

done it before, she'd only seen a film in class and pictures in books and where was that damn doctor, anyway?

"You'd better come inside," Analise called from the doorway. "Echo says it's time."

"But the doctor—"

"Cody? Come inside."

He rushed past her and his brothers and made his way through all the wedding guests to Pauline's room, as it contained the only bed on the ground floor.

He caught himself in the doorway. He'd arrived just in time to see his new sister-in-law, still dressed in her wedding gown, take delivery of a very small, very pink bundle of humanity.

He rushed to Cassie as the baby took a deep breath and let out a holler worthy of every Westin male born on the Open Sky.

"It's a boy," Echo said, as she fussed with the umbilical cord, but he already knew that.

Cody sat abruptly in the chair by Cassie's side and kissed her face a half dozen times. "You're crying," he whispered, as he wiped tears from her cheeks with trembling fingers.

Her soft hand landed on his face. "So are you."

Echo stood over them, their baby in her arms. He was wrapped in the small green and yellow blanket Cody vaguely recalled picking out weeks before. She handed him to Cody, and Cody tilted the baby so both he and Cassie could see their new son's face.

"He looks like you," Cassie said.

Cody couldn't speak. His throat was filled with emotions so varied and so strong they robbed him of a voice. All he could do was stare into the slate eyes of his infant son.

His son.

"I should have known all along you'd turn into a giant marshmallow the minute you saw your baby," Cassie said.

He nodded at her and tried to smile.

"You asked me a question a little while ago," she said. "I was kind of preoccupied at the time, but now I'm ready to answer."

He swallowed the lump and spoke. "Will you marry me all over again, Cass?"

"Yes," she said softly.

He sealed it with a kiss, then cautiously handed her their son. He'd never seen anything as beautiful as Cassie holding her baby.

He was hugging them both when the rest of the family erupted into the room to meet the newest Westin.

* * * * *

SUSPENSE

Heartstopping stories of intrigue and mystery—
where true love always triumphs.

Harlequin®

INTRIGUE

COMING NEXT MONTH
AVAILABLE DECEMBER 6, 2011

#1317 BABY BATTALION
Daddy Corps
Cassie Miles

#1318 DADDY BOMBSHELL
Situation: Christmas
Lisa Childs

#1319 DADE
The Lawmen of Silver Creek Ranch
Delores Fossen

#1320 TOP GUN GUARDIAN
Brothers in Arms
Carol Ericson

#1321 NANNY 911
The Precinct: SWAT
Julie Miller

#1322 BEAR CLAW BODYGUARD
Bear Claw Creek Crime Lab
Jessica Andersen

HICNM1111